Secret of the Pale Lover

Secret of the Pale Lover

Clarissa Ross

Five Star
Unity, Maine

Five Star Romance Series.
Published in 2000 in conjunction with Maureen Moran Agency

The text of this edition is unabridged.

Set in 11 pt. Plantin.

Printed in the United States on permanent paper.

Library of Congress Cataloging-in-Publication Data

Ross, Clarissa, 1912–
Secret of the pale lover / Clarissa Ross.
p. cm.
ISBN 0-7862-2636-6 (hc : alk. paper)
1. Vampires — Fiction. 2. France — Fiction. I. Title.
PR9199.3.R5996 S43 2000
813′.54—dc21 00-035359

Secret of the Pale Lover

Chapter One

For Eve Lewis it began that night in May in the fourteenth-century dungeons of the Caveau des Oubliettes deep in the earth beneath the streets of Paris. There in the eerie underground series of dark chambers came about the experience that was to transform her life. Within the grim shadows of the medieval caves she was to make her first contact with an unknown evil too terrifying to imagine. It was to be the beginning of her involvement with a sinister web of horror in which skeletal hands reached up from the grave to make her one of them.

And yet all this terror had its start at a wild students' party. Eve along with a group of other young men and women from the college had come to this Left Bank bar in the grim dungeon setting to celebrate the end of the term. She was a favorite of the roistering, fun-loving group because she was the only American among them. And because her father had been a French-Canadian and she'd spent much of her girlhood in Quebec, she spoke excellent French. Hence she was apart and yet one of them.

Simon, the young man who was her current romance, circled her with one arm as they sat at the long plank table of merrymakers, and raising his half-empty bottle of red wine in his free hand toasted her, "To Eve, my lovely witch!"

This created additional laughter around the table since it was a joke among them. Eve had come to Paris on a special scholarship to do graduate studies in medieval history of the French provinces, with a special emphasis on the witchcraft and art of black magic peculiar to those misty, far-off days. Although she'd just completed her first year at the college, she was already deeply immersed in her chosen macabre subject. And it was a pet subject of humor among them that she was apprenticing to become a witch.

A pretty blond girl across the table from them shouted above the general bedlam and laughter, "A perfect setting for you, Eve the witch!"

And so it was. The underground bar was dimly lit by flaming torches set out at suitable spots along its dark walls. And the plank tables, plain chairs and giant barrels of wine could have been part of any medieval scene. To complete the weird illusion, the waiters dressed in appropriate style, and chastity belts, thumbscrews and other such relics of the past were set out as decorations around the dank chambers.

Aside from the party of students of which she was a member, Eve saw there were few other patrons in the strange bar at this late hour. The only one who caught her attention was a tall, dignified, elderly man dressed in light gray who sat at a table almost directly under one of the flaring torches, so that it highlighted his gaunt, hawklike features and contoured white hair. She noted that every now and then he regarded their party with some interest.

This was not strange since the students had literally taken over the dungeon bar. The party had become a Bacchanalia as more wine flowed and many of the students became noisily drunken. They now began taking individual turns at entertaining the group. To clapping hands and the lively chant of a popular song, one of the girls mounted the plank table and danced for her wildly applauding friends. A saucy display of shapely bare legs and expert footwork spurred on the students to a new frenzy.

One of the boys from the far end of the table got up and

shouted, "It is time we heard from the witch! We are gathered here in her torture chamber and she has not spoken! Let the witch speak!"

His cry was taken up by the other roisterers, and Eve found herself literally lifted up onto the table. She glanced down at Simon, who gave her an encouraging smile, and amid the laughter and shouting tried to decide what she should do. She mustn't disappoint them at this excited moment.

Her hair was raven black and she wore it loosely at shoulder length. Now she gave her head a toss so that the shining tresses swirled gracefully in place. She lifted her chin proudly, with a knowing smile on the Madonnalike beauty of her lovely face. She had large, luminous green eyes that were her best feature. They sparkled now as, hands at her side, she prepared to address the group. And the sea of faces around the plank table showed expectancy, for she had the reputation of being a madcap.

In the lull that had temporarily come to the reveling group, she spoke out in firm, ringing tones, "I give you Satan and all his coven of witches. All hail Lucifer and may he reign long! May the demons of incubi and succubi give us all pleasure and take us to their fold! I preserve my heart for the Devil, whether he appear in the form of a pretty, handsome Young Man first, or later appeareth in the form of a blackish Gray Cat or Kitling!"

By her spirited declamation she had held their attention with the gibberish she'd chosen at random from among the many incantations she'd read in her studies. Now that she'd finished, she quickly slipped down from the table to sit at Simon's side again to a tumultuous applause.

Someone cried, "I believe she is in league with the Devil!"

This drew more boisterous laughter and a moment later a

young man mounted the table to sing a saucy cabaret tune. One of the waiters had produced an accordion and had come strolling over to the table to provide a musical background for the impromptu soloist. Eve was forgotten by all but Simon in the new excitement. Simon leaned close and kissed her tenderly on the lips.

"If you are a witch, I want to stay under your spell," he told her.

She laughed. She had full red lips and olive skin as a heritage of her dark French-Canadian father. Now she gave her attention to the young man singing. And as he finished one song, he at once began another, and soon the entire group were joining in. The accordionist continued to play, and the mood of the students became more subdued as they began to sing a number of sweet, sad folk songs. Eve was enchanted by the development.

Simon leaned over to her and whispered, "Let's leave before they decide to move on to some other bar. I've had enough."

"So have I," she agreed.

They rose quickly and hurried from the table, while the others were still occupied in their singing. They left the shadowed main dungeon for a darker passageway. They'd gone only a few steps along it when out of the darkness there emerged a stately figure to block their way.

"Mademoiselle Eve, may I take this opportunity of congratulating you on your unusual performance." The voice was elderly and cultured, and she at once recognized the man as the one who'd been sitting at the nearby table watching them.

Embarrassed, she apologized, "Monsieur must think I'm both brazen and mad. It was a prank to amuse our companions."

The white-haired man with the aristocratic hawk face showed a thin smile. "I was impressed by your poise, and the command you held over them all. It almost seemed as if you might have the powers to wield a spell."

Simon, who stood uncomfortably at her side, said, "It is because she is versed in such matters, sir. She is a student of history and black magic at the university."

The tall aristocrat showed interest. "Indeed," he observed. "Then that explains the authenticity of your words. I recognized some of them. I have an interest in the ancient lore myself."

Eve wished he wouldn't keep them standing in the near darkness of the low passageway. She feared the other students would miss them and come trooping after them. And she was weary and wanted to go back to her room for a night's sleep.

But at the same time there was something about this man that fascinated her. A certain hypnotic manner that had caught her attention earlier in the evening. Now as his keen eyes studied her from the shadows, she was uncomfortably aware of the power in them. An eerie face seemed to radiate from those dark pupils to hold her there spellbound.

"Are you truly interested in witchcraft and such," the stranger asked, "or is it merely a course that you are taking for credits?"

She managed a faint smile. "I am interested in my degree, but there is something about the unknown that fascinates me. I'm sure there is more to it than we understand."

The hawk face showed pleasure. "Like myself and the English poet, Milton, you believe, 'Millions of spiritual creatures walk the earth, Unseen, both when we wake and when we sleep.' I'm firmly of that accord."

Young Simon moved uneasily from one foot to another,

and touching her arm said, "They've stopped singing. We'd better go."

"Yes," she agreed, tearing herself away from the hypnotic eyes of the stranger, "we shouldn't wait for them."

The tall man spoke up quickly, "I'm sorry. I didn't intend to detain you. I'd like you to know my name. I'm Count Henri Langlais, and I should like to know yours if I may. It is possible we may sometime meet again when we have time to discuss the things of darkness."

"I'm Eve Lewis," she said, and quickly filled him in on her American background and the fact she was part French. She also introduced him to Simon.

The tall man stood there in the shadows seeming pleased at the information she'd offered him. "Of course you were bound to have some French blood," he told her. "No one could quite so well fit in to this scene otherwise. Do you live in the district?"

Before she realized, she'd given him her address and explained that she was leaving the following day for a two-week holiday in Brittany at a resort town named Dinard.

"But I know Dinard," the tall, white-haired man explained. "You will like the place. I have often gone there myself with my nephew. I'm sure you'll have a pleasant time."

"Thank you," she said politely, aware of the restiveness of Simon at her side. "You will excuse us."

"But of course," he said genially. And he stood there with his hat in hand as they moved along the passageway and left him.

Not until they had emerged in the cool, after-midnight air of the street did Simon remonstrate with her. "You shouldn't have told him so much about yourself."

She stared at the young man in surprise. "But he seemed

very nice. Obviously a gentleman."

The youth frowned. "Don't forget that Paris after dark has many seemingly nice old gentlemen who prey on young girls like you."

Eve halted on the cobblestone street. "You're being far too suspicious. You make him sound like some sort of monster."

Simon's manner was sober. "He could well be one. That underground bar is not the sort of spot you'd expect a titled gentleman to frequent alone."

Her companion had made a telling point. It was rather odd that a man of the Count's years and position should be sitting alone in a Left Bank bar at this hour. And yet it could be through some fluke of circumstance that was not important. He might enjoy the atmosphere. It could be a poignant reminder of places haunted in his youth. She could not picture the friendly, dignified man as a danger.

"He may have had his reasons for being there," she said.

"And he displayed an odd interest in witchcraft and your performance on the table. I don't like it!"

She laughed, and taking the young man's arm, urged him to begin walking again. "Surely you're not jealous."

Simon shrugged. "I'm worried for your safety. Be sure your door is locked tonight. And watch out when you go to Dinard. Those resort towns are filled with all kinds of shady characters."

She smiled at him. "If everyone felt as you do, nobody would go to the seaside."

"You must learn to be less frank and friendly," Simon insisted. "Our young women are far more discreet. You Americans are much too open."

"But I have French blood," she protested. "The Count noticed at once."

"North American French," Simon said moodily, "it doesn't count."

He saw her to the narrow street and quaint old building in which she lived. They talked for a brief period and then he kissed her goodnight. He was remaining in the city for the holidays, but they planned to keep in touch by letter.

Eve unlocked the front door and carefully saw that the latch was in place when she closed it after her. Then she made her way up the winding, dark stairway to the large attic room that had become her home in Paris. In many ways it was like a dream world. The scholarship that had brought her to the French capital had introduced her to an exciting adventure in another kind of living.

Things were much different from at home in Newark. And she was gradually picking up the customs and values of the students with whom she lived and studied. Yet Simon found it possible to point out her American shortcomings. She couldn't see that she'd been indiscreet in telling the Count so much about herself, and she felt the young man had made too much of it.

At the door of her own room on the low-ceilinged top landing, she found her key and let herself in. Remembering Simon's admonition, she was careful to lock it again after her. The room was floodlighted by moonlight that came in through the partly opened, multi-paned windows that overlooked the chimneys and rooftops of adjoining houses. Without bothering with a light, she began to undress for bed.

The meeting with the aristocratic old figure and his obvious familiarity with witchcraft and interest in it continued to interest her. He had claimed to recognize some of the incantations she'd voiced. To do that he must have given time and study to the dark arts. She wished that conditions had been different and she could have sat down with the cultured nobleman and discussed the sorcery and spiritualism of the long ago medieval days.

In her thin, white flowing nightgown she moved to the window to stare up at the moon for a few moments with a questioning look on her lovely face. The dark, shining hair streaming down on her shoulders gave her the appearance of some beautiful maiden of an ancient period. She lost herself in thoughts of that dark other world she was convinced did exist.

For she had not been indulging in mere words when she'd assured Count Henri Langlais that she had definite belief in the supernatural. She could not have delved into her studies of witchcraft if she hadn't held these convictions. Her eyes fixed on the moon, and as she stared at its cool, silvery orb, a vision seemed to cross before her. She was staring into the shadowed, thin face of the Count and his hypnotic eyes, which were superimposed against the moon.

She stood there motionless and staring, and then her lips began to move as she murmured, "Wherever the terrible light shall burn, Vainly the sleeper may toss and turn; His leaden eyes shall he ne'r unclose, So long as that magical taper glows, Life and treasure shall he command, Who knoweth the charm of the glorious Hand!"

Thomas Ingoldsby had written the words in the eighteenth century. The magical taper was the Dead Man's Candle. A candle placed between the fingers of the hand. It was made with a wick of dead man's hair and the oil of a murderer's fat. The Hand of Glory had to be the right hand of an executed murderer. It must be severed from the wrist during the eclipse of the moon. Dried and steeped in preserving salts, the hand could be used in weaving many kinds of spells.

The vision of the Count's hypnotic features vanished as abruptly as it had appeared, and she began to tremble. A cool breeze came in through the partly opened windows and sent a chill running through her. She couldn't understand why she'd suddenly had such macabre thoughts. It wasn't like her. With a tiny frown she pushed the windows closed, went across to her bed and slipped between the sheets.

The room was darker with the curtained windows cutting off some of the moonlight. She lay in bed with the bedclothes drawn up to her chin and stared up into the shadows. She was weary from her studies and needed a holiday. The stay in Dinard would do her good. The Count had spoken of it as a pleasant place and assured her she would like it. He'd also spoken of having visited there often with his nephew.

His nephew! Eve found herself speculating on what sort of person the young man would be. Certainly he would have education and bearing if he were anything like Count Henri. And she would judge the family to be wealthy. The Count had an air of the jaded aristocrat about him. And she thought how interesting it would be to know such a family better. To meet a young man like the Count's nephew.

Since coming to Paris she'd had little contact with the wealthy or upper classes, except those representatives found among the student body. And all students became the same type when grouped together, so there was no opportunity to study social divisions among them. Simon, whom she dated more than most of the boys, was the son of working people. She liked him, but there was nothing serious between them. It was a most casual friendship, and there had been periods when they hadn't seen each other for several weeks. Now that she was leaving Paris for a little, the young man was showing a special interest in her.

But she did not feel bound to him. Or find it necessary to explain her comings and goings to him, or the choice of her friends. For that reason she'd not paid too much attention to his complaints about her being too friendly with the Count. She did not feel he was altogether competent to pass such social judgments. But she did like Simon and would send him some postcards as she'd promised.

The idea of meeting a handsome young aristocrat, as the Count's nephew would be, did thrill her. Perhaps it had been part of her romantic dreams before she'd come to Paris. The reality had proven different from the exotic world she'd envisioned. In many ways her fellow students were quite thoroughly Americanized, and rock and roll and Coca Cola were as much a part of their pattern of living as unwrapped sticks of bread and good red wine.

So she still clung to a dream that the different world she'd looked forward to might exist outside the city. In the smaller provincial towns she pictured fine old castles with benevolent upper-class families ruling the countryside from them. Count Henri Langlais would undoubtedly make an ideal head of a village, and she was sure he must play some role like that.

With these thoughts she slipped off into a sound sleep. But she was to be haunted with frightening dreams as she tossed restlessly under the thin coverings. A dull crimson glow converged on her, and she was standing in this eerie light surrounded by great clouds of steam that floated up about her. In the background there was a weird, moaning sound, like the anguished pleas of tormented souls. The wailing rose and ebbed as the misty billowings blocked out any clear vision of where she was.

And then a sharp pain shot through her wrist, and she drew back with a cry and glanced down to see a bony hand clasped around the wrist! A skeleton hand with no body attached! She twisted her arm in a vain effort to cast the phantom hand off, but it clung, leechlike. And there were horrible tiny spiders running back and forth along the bones of the steely phantom fingers. She screamed in fear that they would scurry up her arm and ran forward. Suddenly she was confronted by an altar, and standing at it in crimson robes was Count Henri Langlais. The aristocratic white-haired man raised a hand and intoned something. At the same instant the skeleton fingers vanished from her wrist.

She knelt down before the altar in tears and told the Count of her frightening experience. He paid no attention to her sobbing and the story of her unhappy torment. He raised his hand again as he went on talking in a strange tongue unfamiliar to her. And she saw the Egyptian magical square, inscribed with numbers, drawn on his palm. There was a dark blob in its center.

Her terrified eyes fastened on the dark smear, and she seemed to be literally drawn into the darkness. Now the sea was roaring in her ears. The angry sound of the surf as it crashed against rocks. She was walking along a deserted beach, and the boulders and the waves were huge to her, as if she were of doll-like size. The sun was hazy and she could see along the beach for what seemed miles.

And then she saw another solitary figure coming towards her. As the dark-clad figure drew nearer, she thought it was the Count again. But it was a younger man with the Count's fine features, but without the lines of age and weariness. He smiled at her, and she was fascinated by his handsome countenance and his wavy blond hair. He had the look of a romantic film actor. She ran up to him and he extended his hands to greet her.

She was ready to clasp his hands when she saw with horror that there were skeleton hands protruding from the coat sleeves, exactly like the horrible hand that had gripped her so cruelly before. She stumbled back with a scream as the hands drew close to clamp onto her.

She was still screaming when she woke abruptly and sat up to adjust to the darkness of her bedroom. It took only seconds for her to be aware of the light tapping at her windows. A persistent eerie tapping that was not the wind nor like anything normal she'd ever heard. Her blood froze as the thought crossed her mind that the soft yet urgent tapping conjured up the specter of skeleton fingers.

She remembered she hadn't properly locked the windows. She'd been careful to mind Simon's admonitions and lock both doors, but she'd merely pushed the windows too carelessly. And while she had an idea the catch had caught a little, it hadn't locked fully. Now she forced herself to stare in the direction of the ghostly tapping, and she saw the windows move just a trifle.

It called for instant action, and she was immobilized by her terror. Somehow she made herself get swiftly from the bed, race to the windows and press them closed with all her strength. She was vaguely aware of something outside bumping against the panes of glass that looked like a huge dark bird. At once her frightened thoughts fastened on a bat. It must be some revolting giant bat out there trying to blindly force an entry into her bedroom.

Despite her panic she held the window tightly shut until the uncanny thing vanished and the tapping and pressure on the window ended. She felt weak and sick, and the perspiration stood out coldly at her temples. What vile thing had been lurking out there?

She was still confused. The frightening reality had come so soon upon her grotesque dreams that one seemed to mix with the other. She began to wonder if she hadn't imagined the tapping at the window, that it had been merely the end of her nightmare. But there had been that continuing pressure as she'd bolstered the window catch with her own strength.

This gave credence to what had been a decidedly eerie interlude.

After waiting a moment, she gingerly opened the hinged windows a little to stare out the crack left between them. And it was then that she caught a glimpse of something that made her hold her breath for a startled second. On a rooftop several houses distant, she caught a fleeting glimpse of a crouched male figure retreating. The dark-clothed figure dodged behind a convenient chimney and she lost sight of him. She stared at the shimmering moon-misted rooftops that were once again empty of movement. Had she really seen someone, or had it been another illusion?

How could she tell? Thoroughly shaken, she closed the windows, and this time latched them with care. She returned to bed, but at least two hours had passed before she was able to drop off into an uneasy sleep once more. And when she did, she slept only a little while. She kept waking with starts. But there were no more alarms. At last dawn showed itself, and only then did she completely relax and sleep soundly.

It was to be expected that she overslept. This meant she had to rise hastily, snatch breakfast and pack for her planned seaside holiday. She tried to force the memories of her nightmare from her mind as she hurried, but they were malevolently persistent. After her unhappy night she was glad to be leaving the room for awhile.

A frantic cab ride to the railway station, and she was at last safely in a compartment aboard the train. She had settled down to enjoy the train trip when the compartment door opened and a bent, parchment-faced old man in shabby black suit, flowing string tie and floppy black felt hat joined her in the otherwise empty compartment.

The newcomer smiled at her, revealing yellowed stumps of teeth, and then took a seat opposite her. He had the cadaverous, hollow-cheeked face of a corpse, and his eyes were sunken and covered with a disgusting film. But it was his hands protruding from the ragged black coat sleeves that drew her reluctant eyes. They were thin and clawlike, the hands of a skeleton!

Like the skeleton hands of her nightmare. She tried to stop staring, but the hands pressed down on the worn velour seat of the compartment held a horrible fascination for her. She felt she could not stay there alone with him and had a compulsion to rush from the compartment and find some other place on the train. But any thoughts she might have had in this direction were curbed by the train whistle blowing and the jolt of the railway carriage as it began the journey. Now she was trapped!

She glanced out the window as the train gathered speed. And she could also see a faint reflection of the cadaverous old man in the window glass. She was sure he was staring at her in an eerie fashion, the mouth gaped open to reveal a dark oval, the eyes holding a malevolent gleam in their filmy depths. She was both disgusted and frightened.

Now the train was clipping along at a fast rate. She began to feel drowsy in the musty atmosphere of the compartment, with the regular rhythm of the wheels pounding into her ears. Once her eyes nearly dropped closed and she sat up with a start. When it happened a second time, she forced herself to move on the seat.

She sat very straight, staring at the old man. He startled her by showing a smile and addressing her in some language she couldn't understand. The words made no sense. She couldn't place what they might be. So she pretended to not have heard him, and he became silent again.

Now she tried to think where she'd heard some similar phrases before. They had seemed to have a haunting ring.

And suddenly she knew. In her nightmare! The Count had addressed her from the altar in similar phrases in her nightmare! Or so it seemed! But of course this was absurd! She was allowing her imagination to run away with her. It just couldn't be possible.

She sat there tautly, and very slowly the drowsiness came back to plague her. She fought it, telling herself that she was caught there with some mad kind of creature. But warning herself that she must be alert for her own protection did no good. Her lack of sleep during the night and the lulling atmosphere of the train's clicking wheels combined to put her to sleep.

She wakened with a gasp! Filled with panic she stared across to see what the old man might be doing now. And he was gone! He just wasn't there any longer. She studied the empty seat in horror. It seemed unlikely the train had stopped during her light dozing spell. Yet somehow he had escaped from the compartment. How could it be possible? And then a horrible thought struck her. How could it be possible unless he were a ghost?

Chapter Two

The rest of her trip to the seaside resort of Dinard was sheer anticlimax. The memory of the horrible old man and his odd disappearance continued to haunt her. It seemed that beginning with the party in the dungeon the previous night, she'd encountered a chain of uncanny happenings. Or was she merely construing perfectly ordinary events in that way because of a state of nerves.

The palms of her hands were sweating profusely, and her head seemed dizzy, this with a dryness of her mouth made her debate whether she had picked up some illness. At last they reached the station at Dinard and she got off the train. She was thankful for the company of a number of others on the platform and found a porter to take care of her luggage and get her a cab.

The resort area of Dinard stretched along a street facing onto a broad wooden boardwalk with a link railing overlooking the wide beach. The type of accommodation ranged from modest rooming houses to great luxury hotels. Eve had chosen her hotel blindly on the basis of price, and it turned out not to be in the luxury class, though it was several levels above the cheap rooming houses.

The proprietor, a dumpy little man with a bald head and walrus mustache, duly registered her and informed her of the hours the dining room was open. This done, he turned her over to a sleepy porter who'd been standing hidden by several large, dusty potted palms. As Eve left the lobby behind the porter, she was regarded with glares by elderly angular females, with interest by one or two semi-decayed, middle-aged husbands, and with blunt audacity by some young children. She decided she would best enjoy her holiday by spending as much time on the beach as possible.

The room smelled of ancient furnishings and salt water in about equal proportions. She tipped the porter, and left alone, sat on the edge of the iron framed bed. Again she had a momentary fainting feeling and clutched the bedspread to brace herself against the spell. It passed, and she decided she would unpack quickly and go to the beach for a swim. The open air and cool ocean would do wonders for her she was sure.

It took more than a half-hour to unpack and change into her white bathing suit. Over it she wore her terry-towel beach dress. With cap in hand and sun glasses hastily found, she left the room and went downstairs. Passing through the lobby was an ordeal once again. The gabble of conversation ceased at her appearance, and staring eyes followed her out the doorway. As she left, she heard the flurry of talk begin once more.

She strode toward the boardwalk with grim determination. She was going to enjoy her holiday no matter what. She speculated on changing to more luxurious quarters, or even to quieter if more modest ones, but flinched at the idea of facing the grumpy little hotel owner and demanding her money back, or that part due to her if she left. She had certain visions of his being difficult, and she really was not feeling well enough to face a scene.

A small flight of steps led down from the boardwalk to the beach itself. She walked along the sand, ignoring the fairly considerable number of holidayers stretched out there. At last she found a suitably quiet spot and doffed her robe to stand and feel the refreshing breezes caress her slim body.

She stood there a moment and then put on her cap and fastened it. Next she went down to the water, let the cold waves touch her toes, and finally waded in.

The water was not too cold and she enjoyed her swim. The feeling of dizziness and nausea had left her, and she came back to the beach refreshed. She had hope that her holiday might not be a disaster after all. Except for meals and the hours of sleeping, she could avoid the stuffy little hotel. She dried her hair and sat on her robe enjoying the sun. Staring down to the left, she saw that the beach was more rocky there and seemed deserted as compared to the wide white sandy stretches on her right, which were crowded with bathers. For awhile she lay on her stomach and let the hot sun blaze down on her back. Her mind returned to the railway carriage, and the weird parchment face of the old man became vivid for her once again.

What had happened to him? Had he ever really existed except in her imagination? How had he managed to vanish so quietly and so quickly? These questions nagged at her. She also recalled the horrible nightmare and its sequel to the bat-like creature trying to make its way into her room. All at once she became fearful and restless and sat up to stare around her. The beach was placid as before.

She felt she wanted to take a walk and had no desire to thread her way among the crowds on the busy section of the beach. Picking up her robe and bag with suntan lotion, she resolutely set out along the deserted, rocky area to her left. The tide was coming in, and the roar of the waves was getting stronger. She'd not gone more than fifty yards before she had a fresh attack of vertigo and halted. She touched a hand to her temple and blinked behind her sunglasses to try and rid herself of the blurring of her eyes.

It must have been a full minute before the weakness

passed. Still not feeling herself, she moved on more slowly until she had left the busy portion of the beach far behind her.

All at once the rocks and sand and sea seemed to form a familiar pattern. She had the strange sensation that she had been there before. Hesitating, she glanced around nervously, conscious of her isolation on this deserted section of the beach. A touch of dizziness came to her again as she began to realize this was the beach she'd walked in her nightmare. Exactly the same one! That was why she'd thought she recognized it.

Fear shot through her and she stood there fighting the weakness that was numbing her again. And then she saw the figure coming around some rocks and walking slowly towards her. A small cry of fear escaped her lips as he came close enough for her to see it was the handsome blond man of her nightmare. It was too dreadful! She swallowed hard as he came nearer, and she recognized the familiar features, a younger edition of the Count, and then she let her terrified eyes drop to a study of his hands. If they were the skeleton hands of her nightmare, she was certain she would faint. And as this frantic thought raced through her brain, everything became confusion and she blacked out.

The face bending over her with a solicitous expression belonged to a stout man of middle-age with a bald perspiring head. "Mademoiselle is better now?" the stranger asked.

Eve stared up at him in bewilderment. "Where has he gone? The blond young man with the bony hands?"

The stout man frowned. "I saw no blond man," he told her. "I came along the beach and found you collapsed on the sand."

With a deep sigh, she said, "He came towards me. I was terrified. That is why I fainted."

The man bending over her looked puzzled. "Did he

threaten you in some way?"

Eve's mind was gradually clearing, and she felt discomfiture. It would be impossible to explain the relation between her dream and her meeting with the young man on the beach. She said, "I must have taken a weak spell."

"You look ill," the man said. "It could be the sun."

She sat up and shook her head. "No. I didn't feel well before I came to the beach."

The stout man had a barrel chest covered with coarse black-gray hair, and wore blue bathing trunks from which emerged bowed hairy legs. He said, "I happen to be a doctor. My name is Devereaux. May I see you safely back to your hotel or boarding place?"

She stood weakly beside him. "My hotel is along the boardwalk not far from here. I'm sure I can manage to get there all right."

The stout man looked dubious. "I wonder," he said. "I'd like to go along with you and see if I can diagnose your trouble."

"I'm afraid I'm inconveniencing you," she apologized.

"I was just out killing time," he said. "Let me accompany you."

Because she still felt badly, she made no strong protest. And when she began to walk, she was unsteady on her feet. He quickly came to her aid and helped her along. By the time she reached the hotel she was exhausted. The doctor had put on an open-necked sports shirt which he'd been carrying and was more presentable for entering the lobby. Their entrance again drew attention from the mixed group sitting around there. Eve was too ill to care much.

When the doctor got her to her room, he felt her head and checked her pulse. "You've picked up a touch of some kind of fever," he announced. "You'd do best to stay in bed for a night and day. I'll send you some pills and the instructions for taking them. It seems nothing serious and you should quickly return to normal."

She smiled at him wanly. "You've been most kind to a stranger. Let me pay you."

The stout man raised a protesting hand. "Not at all. I'm happy to be of some service to a fellow-traveler. If one can't indulge in these small gestures, where is the joy in living?"

He stayed a few minutes more and left her promising that his teenage daughter would bring the pills to her within the hour. As soon as he left, Eve was happy to change and get into bed. She was feeling nauseated again, and when a slim, leggy young girl came and left the tiny bottle of pills, she was barely able to thank her. As soon as the girl left, she took the first of the pills and sank into a deep sleep.

When she awoke, it was after midnight and the room was in darkness. A quiet had settled on the small hotel as she got up and switched on the single light bulb. She felt much clearer in the head and the nausea had left her. But though she'd slept through dinner she was not hungry. She had an idea the strong pills might have dulled any hunger pains.

She saw that it was time to take them again. She did this and returned to bed. This time she slept until the morning. But she was awake in time for breakfast. In spite of the friendly Dr. Devereaux having advised her to rest a full day, she saw no reason for doing so. She went down and was shown to her table in a verandah dining room. The dour waiter informed her she would be sharing the table with a spinster who'd already breakfasted and gone for her morning stroll. Eve was glad of the temporary privacy and enjoyed her breakfast.

Before noon she felt well enough to take a short walk. She hoped that she might see some sign of Dr. Devereaux along the boardwalk, since he was also there on holiday. But a lengthy stroll produced no hint of the stout, pleasant face. In the afternoon she slept again. But she was well enough to go down for dinner and meet the elderly, vinegar-faced spinster who was her table companion.

"You've been missing some of your meals," the thin one sniffed over her soup.

Eve smiled. "I was ill. But I'm over it now."

The spinster looked alarmed. "Nothing catching, I trust."

"I'm sure it wasn't," she hastened to say.

She left the table as soon as she could for another walk. When she returned to her hotel, she heard several of the guests discussing the fireworks exhibition that was being held on the beach after dark. She at once made up her mind to see this. After staying in her room and reading until darkness came, she again went out to join the crowds lining the boardwalk for the fireworks. She moved along until she found a vacant place at the railing and waited.

It was not long before the first colorful rocket shot up into the sky to spread a showering rainbow of sparks. Others followed in a rapid succession of dazzling multicolored splendor and accompanied by many loud reports that made the crowd gasp. Shadowy figures moved quickly along the beach to set off special pieces, such as a horse and carriage, an enchanted palace, a funny motor car, and revolving wheels of red, orange and blue. Eve was enchanted by the display, and when the last rocket had been set off and the colorful "Bon Soir" burned out, she felt let down.

Now she had only the prospect of her shabby hotel for the balance of the evening, and it was not late. She was about to start back when a cultured voice at her elbow called out her name, "Mademoiselle Lewis!"

She wheeled around in surprise to find herself looking into

the smiling face of the aristocratic Count Henri Langlais. She smiled and said, "How nice to see you again so soon."

"I think I mentioned that I often came here," the Count said. "My estate is along the coast only a few miles from here." He turned to a figure standing in the background politely. "I'd like you to meet my nephew, Leonard."

The young man stepped up to take her hand, and she couldn't help gaping in astonishment. It was the young man of her nightmare and the one she'd seen on the beach. He was exactly like the Count, except that his face did not show the lines of aging. When the handsome blond man reached out to shake her hand, she stared down in consternation, expecting to see the skeleton fingers ready to grasp her.

But of course this was not the case. He had a slender, tanned hand that was pleasantly firm as he greeted her. "My uncle told me of his meeting with you," Leonard Langlais said, smiling and revealing perfectly shaped white teeth. "Your interest in the black arts fascinated him. And I'm happy to have this chance of knowing you."

Eve recovered some of her poise. It had been stupid of her to confuse her nightmares with reality. She had merely envisioned this young man as he was likely to be. It turned out that her fantasies had been very close to the truth. He did look like a younger version of his uncle. She stood there with the two well-dressed men as the crowd jostled around them.

"I find the beach with its hordes of people rather overwhelming," Count Henri Langlais said in his patrician way. "Have you any plans for the rest of the evening?"

"Not really," she told the white-haired man. "I was ill yesterday and I remained in my room. Though I'm feeling better now."

His nephew smiled at her. "I must say you look very well."

"Indeed you do," the Count agreed suavely. "Would you

consider joining us in the cafe of our hotel for refreshment and conversation?"

Eve hesitated. The idea was appealing, but she wondered whether she felt up to it. The pills given her by the doctor had miraculously cured her and left her in a relaxed, carefree mood, but she didn't want to risk having a relapse.

"We won't keep you too long," the young man said. "And I'll see you back to your hotel the moment you say."

She smiled. "Very well. For just a little while then."

"Excellent," the Count said. "Now let me see if I can hail a cab to take us to the hotel. We can't remain on the boardwalk to be pushed around by these tourists." He said this with a note of disdain in his cultured voice.

Leonard smiled at her as they were left alone for a moment. "My uncle has a passion for privacy. He enjoys meeting few people. You should be pleased that he is so taken by you."

It was a flattering and rewarding experience. The Count got them a taxi, and within a few minutes they were at the entrance of the Lido, the largest and most luxurious of Dinard's resort hotels. Eve entered the high-ceilinged splendor of the lobby flanked by the two handsome men and feeling as if she'd arrived in a different world. And indeed she had.

They went on to the dimly lighted cafe where an austere headwaiter at once recognized Count Henri and led them to an excellent table with a view of the moonlit ocean. The Count ordered light refreshments for them, and they relaxed around the table with its shaded orange candle flickering to talk quietly.

Eve was fascinated by the manners and elegant dress of the handsome old man and his equally good-looking nephew. They were both excellent conversationalists and able to put her completely at ease.

She told them of her experience in meeting the doctor and of the free medication he'd given her. "I have some of the pills left," she said, "but I'm so much better I don't think I'll take them."

"I would," the Count advised her. "It could prevent you having another attack of whatever strange element it was that took hold of you."

"I suppose you're right," she agreed. "They surely won't harm me since they leave me in such a pleasant mood."

"They could be a type of tranquillizer," Leonard Langlais volunteered. "I have taken them on occasion, and they've helped me a great deal."

"It was silly of me to take ill as soon as I got on the train," Eve said. "I appeared quite well until then."

The waiter came to serve them. After he left, Count Henri Langlais looked at her with a twinkle in his sharp eyes. "The way you invoked the Devil the other night, it could be that this was a curse put upon you."

She smiled. "That was just a joke on my part. I wanted to amuse the party. I don't worry too much about black magic."

The Count's hawk face showed a mocking look. "You'd be wise to give it some thought. Surely you've come upon the curse of the Sword of Moses?" The flame of the candle played its light on the aristocratic face and gave it an eerie, ghostly appearance as he leaned close to recite in a low voice, "I call thee, evil spirit, cruel spirit, merciless spirit. I call thee, bad spirit, who sittest in the cemetery and takes away healing from man. Go and place a pain in her head, in her eyes, in her mouth, in her tongue, in her throat, in her windpipe. Put poisons within her, I will send you the evil angels Puziel, Guziel, Psdiel, Prziel. I call thee and those six pains that you go quickly to her and kill her, because I wish it. Amen. Selah."

A weird silence settled on the table as he finished and stared at her expectantly. Awe filled her lovely face. She stared from him to his nephew and saw that the handsome face of the blond young man had taken on an odd absent look, his eyes seemed to have dulled and he was staring off into the distance. She broke the quiet by uttering a tiny gasp.

"You know that ancient curse by heart," she told the Count. "I'm familiar with it from some of my textbooks, but I've never memorized it."

The elderly man smiled grimly. "I told you sorcery was a hobby of mine."

"And you're well versed in it," she exclaimed. She glanced at his nephew now and saw that he had lost his odd expression and seemed to be normally listening to what was being said. She asked him, "Do you also have some knowledge of the supernatural?"

"Enough," Leonard said. "But my uncle is the expert."

Eve smiled for the Count's benefit. "I shall protect myself against your curse by the ancient charm: Black luggie, hammer-head, Rowan-tree and red thread, Put the warlocks to their speed."

The Count wore that mocking look again. "That's a famous charm against evil," he agreed. "Though I'm not sure I like your hinting that I'm a warlock, I've never been called a male witch by anyone before."

She laughed. "I'm just trying to prove that I have a sound foundation in witchcraft."

"And you have," Leonard spoke up. "But surely there must be more pleasant topics for us to discuss. Do you play tennis, Miss Lewis?"

"Please call me Eve," she told him. "And I do play tennis. I have my racket with me. Unfortunately my hotel doesn't seem to have courts."

"We have several excellent ones here," the young man said. "And we shall have a game tomorrow."

"How long are you going to be here?" Eve asked.

The young man glanced at the Count. "How long?"

Count Henri Langlais made no direct reply but instead asked her, "How long will you be here, Eve?"

"Two weeks."

"Strange," the Count said. "That is exactly the same period we've booked. So you and my nephew will have plenty of time together."

Leonard gave her a warm glance. "I'm looking forward to our holiday," he said.

For Eve it made everything different. She knew she could endure the second-rate hotel she was staying in as long as she had the delightful company of Leonard and his uncle. And they were being extremely generous in inviting her to share the luxuries of their expensive resort. Her holiday in Dinard was going to be a success after all.

As good as his word, Leonard saw her home as soon as she mentioned feeling weary. He took her to the hotel in a cab, and they had their first goodnight kiss at its entrance in the moonlight. As he let her go, she stared up at the full moon and was suddenly aware of an unusual dark shadow on it.

In an excited voice, she told him, "Look! There's an odd shadow on the moon. Almost a bat shape."

He glanced around quickly and there was a hint of fear on his handsome profile as he stared up at the silver orb suspended above the ocean. "I don't see it," he said.

"But you must!"

"Sorry," he told her in a rather grim tone. "I don't seem to have your imagination."

She looked up at the moon again. "It's still there."

The young man offered her a wan smile. "I forget you have

an affinity with the dark world," he said. "I'll leave you to your black clouds and the moon."

She went into the hotel as he rode off in the taxi. As she mounted the stairs to her room, she decided that she liked the Count's nephew even though she didn't fully understand him. He had those baffling moments when he seemed to withdraw or be on the defensive about something unimportant. His reaction to her remark about the moon just now had been an example.

When she reached her room, she took another glance at the moon from her window. And strangely the shadow or cloud that had resembled a bat had moved from the face of the moon. There was no sign of it any longer. She prepared for bed in a satisfied mood and followed the Count's instructions to take another dose of Dr. Devereaux's pills. She made up her mind to search the beach for the friendly doctor again. But she didn't think she'd have time in the morning, for she'd agreed to play tennis with Leonard and he was picking her up fairly early.

Again she had a restful sleep and woke to the bright sunshine of another day with the glowing feeling of goodwill the pills seemed to induce. She took another one and saw that she had enough to supply her for several more days if she followed the doctor's note.

At ten sharp Leonard came by in a sleek gray sports car. She slid in on the seat beside him and again was fascinated by his tanned good looks and wavy blond hair. They drove to his hotel and the tennis courts and had a wonderful morning topped by lunch on the hotel balcony with his uncle joining them.

Count Henri Langlais mostly kept to himself and gave her plenty of time in the younger man's company to get to know him well. The days were filled with swimming, boating and tennis. And the nights were a round of dancing spots and the roulette tables. Eve had never known such a wonderful holiday in her life.

Occasionally in the evenings when Count Henri Langlais was with them, he'd talk to her seriously about witchcraft and the black arts. He revealed a vast fund of knowledge on the subject that made her feel like the amateur she was.

The days and nights went swiftly by, and Eve forgot about all her nightmares and apprehensions. Both men were charming to her, though Leonard occasionally relapsed into a tense and almost sullen mood. She tried to overlook this since he was so pleasant in other respects.

She sent several cards to Simon in which she said she was having a grand time, though she was discreet enough not to mention she'd met the Count again and had been almost constantly in the company of his nephew. Simon's single letter to her had been filled with warnings to be careful of her behavior at the beach resort. She began to think he was a dull, unimaginative fellow whom it would be best to avoid in the future.

She finished the pills left her by Doctor Devereaux and never did set eyes on the friendly stout man again. She decided that he must have left the resort town almost as soon as they'd met. Otherwise she would have been certain to have seen him. At any rate, his pills had done their work and she continued to feel remarkably well.

Soon there were only two days left of her vacation. As she and Leonard sat on the beach in their bathing suits the next to their last day, he suggested, "Why don't we go out to St. Malo tomorrow?" And he told her of the quaint spot with its ancient fishing village and old monastery, and of how at low tide you could reach it by land, but when the ocean came rushing back at high tide it became an island. "A suitable excursion for our last day," he said.

She agreed that it would be a pleasant adventure. And he promised to come by for her at nine the next morning. Meanwhile, that night, the Count gave them a special dinner in the main dining room of the hotel. They had a table in a suitably remote corner of the room and a special selection of food and wines.

Once during the dinner Leonard went to take a long distance call that he'd mentioned he was expecting. This left the Count alone with Eve for a little, and he took the opportunity to tell her, "I'm grateful for what you have done for my nephew."

She smiled. "He's made my holiday very pleasant."

"And you have helped him. I've never seen him in such a healthy state of mind and body."

"He strikes me as being a healthy person," she said.

Count Henri Langlais frowned. "As a matter of fact, he's had periods of serious illness. The last bout came about a year and a half ago. As a result he had to limit his activity and take a great deal of rest."

"Yet he's so active now."

"If the ailment does not return, he'll be able to lead a completely normal life," the older man said. "But I live in the shadow of his having another attack. And so does he."

"What sort of illness is it?" she asked.

The Count hesitated. "It is a disease of the blood."

She showed concern. "That can be dreadfully serious."

"Yes. It's not of a malignant nature, thank goodness. It is more a family weakness. The best medical advice we've had claims it to be hereditary. There are no victims for generations but then it crops up again. It is my sincere hope that modern medicine has saved my nephew. And that he will have no recurrence of the condition." He hesitated. "I call the disease the family curse."

"Not in the sense of a true curse."

"Why not? Witchcraft is a reality," he said. "And I consider it to be a possibility that some evil spell was directed towards one of our ancestors and has been passed on through the various generations."

Eve considered and frowned. She was surprised to find this educated nobleman such an avowed believer in the supernatural. She considered what sort of argument she might offer based on her own knowledge of the black arts. "As I understand it," she said, "such spells or curses are usually accompanied by some sinister powder or drug administered to the doomed person. Is it likely your ancestor would accept such a powder or potion?"

"Not if he or she were aware of it," Count Henri Langlais said with a strange expression on his hawk face. "But usually the evil potion is given to the innocent in food or drink, or even in the guise of medicine. So to successfully produce the wicked spell is really not at all that difficult."

Chapter Three

It was the morning of the last day of her vacation in Dinard. Eve went down to the sidewalk in front of the hotel wearing shorts, blouse and sunglasses to await the arrival of Leonard. He had promised to come at nine so they would have plenty of time to explore St. Malo. She carried a bag with her bathing suit and other necessities for the beach. It was a lovely, sunny day, and she looked forward to the adventure with the young man she had come to like so much.

The previous evening had been an interesting one, and she'd been fascinated by Count Henri's revelations about the supernatural. The elderly handsome man was extremely well versed in the rites of sorcery and had talked learnedly of werewolves and vampires. She knew that this rugged section of France and Middle Europe had been the setting for some weird manifestations of this sort.

As she stood there in the increasingly warm sun, the street began to be busier. More people appeared to stroll along the boardwalk and head for the beach. She glanced at her watch and saw that it was almost ten o'clock. She'd been waiting for the young man almost an hour and she'd never known him to be late before.

She at once began to wonder if something had happened and whether he had left a message for her. She went back into the lobby with its usual collection of curious tourists and made her way to the desk. The manager's wife, a sour, swarthy woman was on duty, and seeing Eve approach, the woman glared at her defensively.

Eve asked, "Have there been any phone messages this morning for Miss Eve Lewis?"

"No, Mademoiselle," the woman's reply was emphatic.

"Are you sure?"

The swarthy woman shrugged and turned her back on her. Eve saw she was going to get nowhere with her. Ignoring the stares of the dried-up females and their wizened male counterparts about the dusty potted palms, she went out to the freedom and sunlight of the street again. A frown marred her pretty face as she looked anxiously for some sign of Leonard.

But there was no sign of him or the jaunty sports car. After standing there a moment or two longer, she decided the only way she could get any information about him was to take a cab to his hotel and inquire there. She had no doubt he'd tried to get in touch with her and failed. Communication at her own hotel was hopeless.

It took a little time to find a taxi. So it was almost ten-thirty when she strolled into the lobby of the fashionable resort where Count Henri and his nephew were staying. The atmosphere was quietly pleasant, and the big lobby was almost empty of people. She went up to one of the several clerks behind the main desk and inquired for Leonard.

The clerk asked her to wait a moment while he consulted the guest list. She stood by the desk becoming increasingly uneasy. Before long he returned with an apologetic air.

"Regrets, Mademoiselle," he said. "But Count Henri Langlais and his nephew checked out of the hotel late last night."

She looked at him in astonishment. "Are you sure?"

"There is no question of it."

"Did they leave any messages? My name is Eve Lewis. Is there any letter here addressed to me?" She couldn't believe that after all their kindness they would depart in this unorthodox fashion without a word. Especially not when Leonard had an appointment with her.

The clerk made a brief search for messages and came back with a negative reply. She managed to thank him and then walked away from the desk feeling stunned. What could have happened?

She walked along the boardwalk in the direction of her own small hotel in a dazed and dejected state. She could not accept that the charming Count Henri and his equally pleasant nephew had coldly snubbed her on reaching a hasty decision to leave. She was sure they had called her hotel and left a message, which had been received with the usual lack of interest on the owner's part, and forgotten. It had to be that!

She continued walking slowly, oblivious of the others on the busy boardwalk. And she conjured up reasons that might have made the two leave in a hurry. There could have been some emergency at the chateau. A sudden illness on the part of some relative or friend; even an unexpected death or a fire or accident could have summoned them back. There must be a good reason. Count Henri had her Paris address and surely she would hear from him in due time.

The disappointment and humiliation shadowed her last day at the resort town. She went to the beach alone and swam briefly. Most of the afternoon she spent sitting in the sun. Then, when she sat up to apply some extra suntan lotion to her body, she had an unusual experience. Her gaze wandered to the boardwalk, and she snapped out of the lethargy induced by the hot sun to become suddenly alert. For leaning against the railing of the boardwalk, watching her, was the missing Dr. Devereaux!

She was sure she recognized the dumpy man in white suit and Panama hat as the elusive doctor. At once she sprang to her feet and waved to him. He gave no hint of having noticed her as he went on studying the beach. Frustrated and excited, she dropped the tube of suntan lotion and ran up the beach to the steps leading to the boardwalk. She was breathless as she reached the spot where he'd been standing, but now there was no sign of him. She stood there despairingly as the sea of people moving in both directions jostled by her. Vainly searching the mass of faces, she was unable to spot him. In a crowd such as filled the boardwalk at this peak time of day, it wasn't strange.

What did bother her was the fact he'd ignored her waving to him and not bothered to wait and speak with her. Assuming it had been the doctor. She had only seen him that one time before and he'd been in his bathing suit. Yet she was almost positive the face of the man at the railing had belonged to Dr. Devereaux. Unable to stand the buffeting of the crowd, she made her way back to the steps and the beach. It was another unexplained mystery.

She was forced to book a crowded second class compartment for her journey back to Paris. It was hot in the tiny space with so many people and several times she felt faint. At last they arrived in the city and she found a cab to take her to her attic room in the Left Bank. The interval of her vacation had served to erase the memory of the troubled night she'd spent there before leaving. And the familiar room with her small array of possessions was cheering after the bleak hotel.

While she'd enjoyed her holiday in Dinard, it had left her with a strange feeling. She asked herself if she'd done anything to offend the Count and his nephew, and could think of nothing. It had to be some sort of misunderstanding. She would surely hear from them soon.

She settled down to a routine of study in preparation for her next term. And in her reading she came upon the account of a woman in the village of Langlais who'd been accused of using witchcraft to create discord and evil. She denied the charge, insisting that while she worked spells, it was only for good deeds, such as curing sick animals and people, removing curses from the fields, stables and houses, and so on. She used salt to work her magic, ordinary salt that she infused with power through incantations. Her accusers argued that she had been responsible for the deaths of three young women of the village and attacks on many more. On all those attacked there had been teeth-marks of a weird nature on the throat. The woman was said to be a vampire, but the debate came to an end when she was found murdered in her cottage with the same kind of odd teeth marks on her throat. The mystery surrounding the incidents was still unsolved. The murderer had not been found, and several psychic researchers who had visited the old woman's cottage and the area agreed that the area had been a setting for black magic activities. This had all taken place approximately three years ago.

Eve read and reread the account. She found it odd that in all his talk about the dark arts the Count had chosen to refrain from mentioning this incident. It must be prominently in his mind since it had happened in his own village. Could he have possibly overlooked it for the very reason that it was so familiar? He'd forgotten she wouldn't know about it. She decided this must be the answer.

But Simon, the young student at the university, whom she was seeing again occasionally, took a different view of it all. He chose to consider the Count and the Count's actions as definitely open to suspicion. It was a matter they often argued over coffee at a sidewalk cafe near her place.

Simon frowned at her across the table. "I don't like the sound of it at all. I'm sure neither this Count nor his nephew are what you believe them to be."

She eyed him with a mocking smile. "Nor are they the scoundrels you suggest. What reason would they have to be so nice to me if they weren't respectable people?"

"I can think of many," Simon said darkly. "And you can consider yourself lucky to have escaped without any worse experience than their deserting you at the last moment. Probably the police were after them and they had to make a break for it."

"Why should the police want them?"

He shrugged. "They could be thieves, white-slavers, bogus-check experts. Anything!"

"That's nonsense," she protested. "You have a small middle-class mind. The Count is a well-known gentleman with a title, a village in his family name, and a fine chateau."

Simon became angry. "There may be a Count Henri Langlais with a chateau, a village to squire, and a nephew, but it doesn't have to be the man you know. I think that handsome gentleman you met in the Caveau des Oubliettes is an imposter."

"And I think you're merely being jealous!" she'd retorted.

"We shall see," Simon said.

So when the special delivery letter came one morning with the postmark of Langlais and the Langlais crest on the back of the elaborate envelope sealed with wax, Eve had a moment of triumph. She could scarcely wait to rip open the elegant blue-gray envelope and read the letter on the engraved stationery inside.

The letter was from Leonard Langlais!

It read, "My Dearest Eve: Surely you must think me and my uncle the most thoughtless of men. I find it hard to explain our sudden departure from Dinard. The truth is that when I left the hotel there, I was far from myself. After leaving you I went back to have a short talk with my uncle before retiring. While I was with him, I was stricken with my old illness.

"I believe you have been fully informed as to its nature. No doubt I overdid my exposure to the sun. At least that is what our local doctor says. I have been very unwell, but I'm now on the mend. It is the wish of both Uncle Henri and myself that you should come to visit us at the chateau. Not only will you find the country interesting, but this area is rich in legend. I have many things of a personal nature I would like to discuss with you.

"Please write as soon as possible and let us know if you can come down here for a month or so. And tell us your arrival date so either my uncle or I can be at the station to meet you. Sincerely, Leonard."

Eve put down the letter with a happy smile. Her friends had been vindicated, and the episode was ending in a pleasant way. So much for Simon and all his ridiculous talk about them being undesirables. A combination of things made her desire to accept their kind invitation to go to Langlais for a month. Chief among them was her wish to see the ailing Leonard again, but she also wanted to make a study of the legends of the area in relation to witchcraft. She felt certain it would be of help at the university.

She wrote a reply by return mail and said she would leave in a week. She planned to arrive on a Monday afternoon. Within the span of a few days, an answering letter came back to her along with a tiny box containing an exquisite cameo in black and white. The cameo of a delicate feminine head had a gold scroll frame and case and a chain of gold so it could be used as a pendant.

The note with the lovely gift was brief and written in the different hand of Count Henri Langlais. It said: "Please accept this small token of my great regard for you. Leonard is under the weather today so I'm writing for him. I shall be at the railway station to meet you on Monday."

The letter and gift pleased Eve, though she was concerned about this further indication that the young man she had come to like so much was suffering another relapse. Standing before her dresser mirror, she placed the cameo pendant about her neck. It looked as lovely as she'd hoped.

She reached for the unfamiliar clasp to take the pendant off again when she somehow lost her grip on the slender golden chain and the lovely pendant dropped to the hard boards of the floor. She gave a tiny cry of annoyance and bent to pick it up. As she did so, she was startled to see that the back of the cameo had sprung open in the fall, and now a revolting hairy spider was emerging from it.

Hardly able to believe her eyes, she made no effort to withdraw her hand. In a lightning movement, the many wiry legs of the spider quickly moved onto her hand, and in the next moment she felt the pain of its stinging her. Horrified, she came out of her daze and shook the spider off her hand and jumped up. It scurried across the broad, ancient floorboards and vanished under a chest that sat close to the floor. She watched it disappear with alarm, and now the pain of its bite was shooting up her right arm. In a state of panic she rushed out of the room and downstairs. Reaching the street, she headed for a small pharmacy located on a corner not far from her house.

It was a seedy little shop that she'd passed many times but never entered. She'd patronized one of the drug stores that specialized in American drugs. But now she had no time or choice. Reaching the small shop, she entered the door with its warning bell for the proprietor. The shadowed room smelled of a combination of pungent odors, and the shelves behind the plain counter were dark and empty-looking. The pain in her arm had changed into a dull, burning throb, and she thought it had become red and swollen at the wrist.

After a seemingly endless wait, there was the creak of a floorboard from behind a shaggy green drape, and an ancient face peered around the drape at her. The sight of the old man coming forward to the counter gave her a start. The parchment face and bent shoulders were identical to those she'd seen before. The elderly pharmacist was the double of the ghostly old man who'd frightened her in the train compartment and vanished mysteriously.

"Yes, Mademoiselle?" the old man questioned her.

"I was bitten by some kind of ugly spider," she said. And going on to explain the details, she held out her inflamed hand with the bite itself a brilliant red spot now.

The old man studied the bite with rheumy eyes for a moment and then nodded as if to say he understood. He vanished behind the green drape to the room in the rear, and after a long delay came back again with a small bottle of colorless liquid and a hypodermic. He carefully filled the hypodermic, and then, coming close, injected the fluid into her arm. After which he swabbed the bite with the same liquid. Closing the bottle with trembling fingers, he gave her a knowing look.

"You will recover," he promised. And he named his small fee.

The injection had made her feel better at once. She paid him and hastily left the strange little shop. She remembered that it was closed a good part of the time, and that once when she'd stopped by to get something, the door had been locked. Retracing her steps to her room she found herself feeling a trifle dizzy.

She sat on the edge of her bed for a moment until her head cleared a little. Then she went over and knelt to retrieve the cameo. She was sure the spider had emerged from it, although it was possible that the evil creature had been on the floor near it and she'd not noticed it until the cameo fell. Then it had moved onto her hand.

Examining the pendant, she found that it had not been damaged. The back had sprung open and seemed to make a small chamber behind the cameo itself, though she didn't believe the spider had been in there. She clicked it in place and once again admired the beauty of the piece before she carefully placed it in her jewelry box.

Because she was suddenly feeling sleepy, she stretched out on the bed and pulled the spread over her. Within seconds she had sunk into a weird kind of drugged slumber. Perspiration came out over her body in tiny beads, and she tossed to right and left with her hands upraised on the pillow and clenching at the air as she suffered through an eerie nightmare.

She was back to the night in the room when there had been a strange tapping on her windows. Again she rushed over to hold them tight against the intrusion of some unknown horror. But this time enormous strength was used to press the windows inward, and she could not keep them shut. Very gradually, she had to allow the sections to come open and reveal a huge spider. The monstrous creature was like the one she'd seen on the floor, magnified many times. And it landed on the floor of her room with a dull thud, evil eyes glinting at her. She screamed her terror and drew back hastily as the hairy menace came slowly towards her. She had reached the wall and could retreat no more, and as the horror came closer she screamed again and again.

She awoke wild-eyed and terrified to see that it was pitch dark in her room. As it gradually came to her that she'd been sleeping and had a dreadful nightmare, she lifted herself from the bed and found the light. It was after three in the morning. She stood there weakly and then became conscious of soft sounds against her window. They gave her a start, and she went over quickly to discover her fears had been aroused by nothing more than raindrops. It was beginning to storm, and a series of heavy drops were pelting against the tiny panes of glass.

With a weary sigh, she undressed and went back to bed. The balance of the night was uneventful. She slept late into the morning, and when she rose she felt more like herself. Her arm was no longer inflamed and the red of the bite did not show. It was still raining. When she finished breakfast, she thought it might be wise to visit the pharmacist a second time and discover if he felt her arm needed further treatment.

She put on her raincoat and took her umbrella. In the street she needed them both. There were not many people out because of the storm, and when she reached the ancient pharmacy, she found its door padlocked as it had been on that other occasion when she'd stopped there. It had been a lucky accident that it had been open yesterday. While she didn't think she needed further treatment, she would have liked to ask the old man if he'd been the one on the train. He had looked exactly the same, and she might have been able to find a satisfactory explanation of his vanishing from the compartment.

Standing by the pharmacy door, she considered what she'd do next. Then a tall, thin man in the apron of a grocer showed himself in the doorway of the shop next to the pharmacy.

"The pharmacy is closed, Mademoiselle," he called out to her.

She moved along the brick sidewalk to stand before him. "When will it open?"

The thin man looked puzzled. "It won't, Mademoiselle. It is never open these days."

Eve was startled. "But I was in there yesterday."

The thin man stared at her and then seemed to understand. "But of course, Mademoiselle. The shop was open for a little yesterday. I was in the back finding something."

She nodded. "And the old man who operates it looked after a spider bite I'd gotten."

The thin man again looked shocked. "But that is impossible."

"Oh?" A thin band of fear was tightening in her.

The man in the apron was staring at her suspiciously. "No one operates the shop any more. Its shelves are empty. They have been since my uncle's death!"

Eve's mouth dropped open. "But there was some old man there. He gave me an injection."

The grocer looked both fearful and annoyed. "You must be mistaking it for some other shop, Mademoiselle. I was the only one in there yesterday. And I only had the door open for a half-hour. The shop is empty!" And he turned and quickly went inside.

She stood there in the rain, stunned and embarrassed. The grocer plainly thought she was insane or a troublemaker, perhaps both. She glanced toward the dusty windows of the locked pharmacy and realized that he must have told her the truth. The shop no longer was in use.

"Since my uncle's death!" The words repeated in her mind. Had she seen a ghost yesterday? While the grocer rummaged in the rear of the shop, had a ghost come forward to treat her? It began to seem so. She had never known this confusion before. It was almost as if some curse or evil spell had been placed on her and the old man she'd seen for a second time was part of the supernatural horror.

She trudged back to her room in the rain, uncertain of everything. She began to wonder if she hadn't experienced some kind of hallucination the previous day. She had merely imagined the druggist behind the counter and the injection. It had all been part of the delirium brought on by the spider's bite. The delirium that had lasted through most of the night.

It had to be that, or she had seen and talked to a ghost. Because of her investigations of the spirit world and the statements sworn to by many, she had no doubt it was possible she'd been served by the dead pharmacist. Yet the theory of delirium seemed more likely an explanation.

Because of the macabre nature of these events and the fact she didn't want to tell Simon she'd received a present from the Count, she refrained from giving him an account of what had happened. And as the day drew near for her journey to the distant Brittany village of Langlais, she put the whole affair aside and concentrated on her traveling preparations.

She shared the train compartment with two charming elderly ladies who were journeying to a more distant point in Brittany to visit a cousin. She was grateful for their company and enjoyed their quaint talk. So when the train stopped at the tiny Langlais railway station and she got out, she felt she was saying farewell to friends.

There was no time for her to feel lonely. The moment she stepped down onto the wooden platform of the station, the aristocratic Count Henri Langlais came towards her. He was wearing a brown tweed suit and matching soft hat with a broad brim and looked the country squire. He doffed his hat, and taking her hand in his, touched his lips to it in a courtly gesture.

"I'm delighted to see you, Eve," he said, his hawklike yet handsome face lighted by a smile.

"I had a pleasant journey," she said.

"And your holiday with us shall be pleasant as well," the white-haired man assured her.

She glanced around as the train drew away from the station and saw the sleepy village nearby. It seemed to consist chiefly of one main street of small shops. In the distance were wooded hills. An unexplainable feeling of loneliness surged through her as if she'd heard a deep sighing. For the first time she thought about how isolated this village was and how completely she was trusting herself to comparative strangers. And as soon as she had the thought, she blamed it on Simon's dark talk.

The Count had put on his hat again and was directing a huge burly man in a chauffeur's uniform to gather up her luggage and place it in the car. He turned to her, "Raol is a good servant but rather stupid and clumsy. Still, he drives very well, and it is difficult to secure proper help these days even in an area like this."

Eve and the Count got into the big sedan, and the stolid Raol shut the door and got behind the wheel. Eve watched him with a certain amount of fascination. He moved in a slow robot fashion, and his square, brutish face with small black eyes seemed to never show expression. The drive to the chateau began, and the Count talked pleasantly as they went along narrow wooded roads.

She said, "When I was in Paris, I read something about a witch-hunt that went on here about three years ago. And that the woman who was suspected of being a vampire was murdered and her killer never found."

Count Henri Langlais received her words as if they'd come as an unpleasant shock. His first reaction was to say, "I had no idea the incident had been given that much publicity."

"There was quite a long newspaper account," she said. "I assumed you would know the woman and all the facts because of your interest in the subject."

The white-haired man scowled. "Mother Leger! She has been as much a nuisance dead as she was alive."

Eve was surprised at the attitude he was taking. "I hope you'll forgive my bringing the subject up," she said, "but I wondered why you hadn't spoken of her in our discussion of the supernatural."

The Count gave her a thin smile. "I fear the case was far too ordinary for me to give it much thought. A stupid old woman pretending to have powers that were not hers. She had the newspaper people over-running the village."

"Wasn't she murdered?"

"By a vindictive relation who believed she'd cheated him of some property," he said bitterly. "He vanished from here and so didn't stand trial. But I hold him guilty of the crime."

"What about the girls who were supposedly killed by a vampire? And those who were merely attacked?"

"Hysterical nonsense!" the Count snapped. "It doesn't take much to make these peasant girls imagine they're victims of the supernatural. They are weaned on ghost stories. And those that died were probably murdered by some jealous youth who made it appear the deaths were caused by a vampire."

"I see," she said. "Newspapers do tend to exaggerate."

"Exactly," the Count agreed.

At the risk of annoying him, she felt she should mention the cameo and the vicious black spider that had emerged from it. She said, "The cameo you sent me was lovely. But I had a weird experience as a consequence of it. It fell and opened, and a horrible black spider was inside it."

"Really?" he stared at her as if he found this hard to believe.

"It bit me," she went on. "And my hand became terribly inflamed. It made me really ill."

"Spider bites can be dangerous," the Count agreed sympathetically. "I can't imagine how this could have happened. Do you suppose the spider might have been on the floor, and you didn't notice it until the cameo fell?"

It was a possibility she'd considered and dismissed. But since she knew what he suggested might be true, she decided to agree with him. "That's probably what happened," she said.

"I fear you've found this a long and tiresome road," the Count said. "But we're near the end of it now. We've come to the gate."

She stared ahead and saw there was indeed a high iron gate of ancient design blocking the road. She said, "You have the grounds fenced?"

"A necessity in these days of expert thieves and with the castle containing so many priceless antiques. The entire estate is bordered by a nine-foot-high wire fence charged with electricity at all times. Only the steep cliffs facing the ocean are not guarded. And they offer a natural defense."

"I hadn't thought of the danger of thieves," she admitted.

"I'm afraid we constantly think of it," the Count said with a sigh as the car came to a halt and a husky young man acting as guard unlocked the gates and allowed them to drive through.

As soon as they entered, the gates were closed behind them. But Eve was paying more attention to the picturebook beauty of the scene ahead. The Chateau Langlais sat on a high hill reached by a winding road. It was built of gray stone in a medieval style with many turrets. To Eve it embodied all the huge ancient brooding castles she'd encountered in her research reading. She was sure there must be many eerie stories connected with it.

At her side the Count said quietly, "No one can enter or leave the grounds without our being aware of it."

Chapter Four

The Count's words shattered her reverie. For a moment she felt a chill of fear and isolation. As if the fence around the estate that the man at her side had mentioned suddenly constituted a prison for her. But that was being silly! Managing a small smile she turned to him.

"I hope you don't keep too tight a rein on your guests," she said.

"Never fear," he told her. "Guests and the family come and go at will."

That satisfied her and she began to wonder about Leonard. "How is your nephew's health?" she asked.

"He's improving. But he still must rest a good deal. He always manages to join us at dinner. And he spends some time with us in the evenings."

"It must be trying for him," she said. "He's normally so active."

"Yes," the Count said.

"What do the doctors say?"

The old man shrugged. "The usual thing. They won't commit themselves. But I see improvement in him every day. And I'm sure that merely seeing you again will be better for him than any doctor. I'm sure you know he became extremely fond of you at Dinard."

Eve blushed. "I like him."

"He was worried that we had to leave so suddenly without advising you. But his illness upset everything."

"Of course it would," she agreed. They had now come

close to the great chateau, and she was able to grasp its size and see how many stories it rose in the air. She said, "It's such a large place."

"And very old."

"It has to be."

"We've tried to adjust our modern living to it," the Count said. "Both Leonard and we have separate apartments in different wings of the building. You will be meeting Maria, my wife, and my secretary, Therese Gallant."

Mention of the women cheered her. She had not heard the Count refer to a wife before and had almost assumed him to be a bachelor. At least there would be female company in the great mansion. In spite of the storybook look of the chateau, she had an idea that life there would be quite normal and the inhabitants pleasant people.

She said, "The chateau must be very old indeed."

"It is," he said, "and it comes complete with suits of armor, fine old tapestries, valuable relies of the past, and even a torture chamber in the cellar, which you shall see."

Eve smiled. "And does the estate also have a ghost?"

"More than one," the Count said with a mocking look on his handsome lined face. "But you are bound to know more about that later."

They arrived at the front entrance of the chateau. Broad granite steps led up to an arched oak door. The moment the car stopped, the door opened and an elderly butler in black and a housekeeper of equally mature age came out to greet them and get her bags. Raol lumbered out of the car and held the door open. The Count emerged first and then helped her from the sedan. As she stepped out onto the gravel, she briefly looked into the face of the burly Raol and was slightly upset to see his beady, black eyes were fixed on her with greedy interest.

The Count gave brief directions to his servants and led her into the large reception hall. As soon as she entered the shadowed room, she was conscious of the cool and the odor of great age. True to her guide's prediction, she saw a coat of armor mounted in a dark corner. The Count took her through the hall and down a corridor.

"My wife and Therese will be in the rear parlor," he informed her, his words hollowly echoing in the quiet house with its stone floors and tall ceilings.

They came to an open door, and inside in a pleasant living room, she saw seated in highbacked chairs a matronly, gray-haired woman and an attractive redhead. They both stood up as she and the Count came into the room.

The Count said, "This is Mademoiselle Eve Lewis of whom Leonard and I have so often spoken."

The gray-haired woman gave Eve a smile. She had a sad face and very white skin. "Welcome to the Chateau Langlais," she said.

"Thank you," Eve said quietly.

The Count turned to the red-haired girl who had been studying Eve with appraising eyes. Now she stood there with a rather defiant expression on her pretty though arrogant face. She wore a black miniskirt and white silk blouse of low cut.

The Count introduced her as "Therese Gallant, my secretary, and the only daughter of a dear dead friend."

Therese bowed coolly to Eve and said nothing. For no reason Eve could immediately think of, the redhead seemed to have an instant dislike for her. And then she remembered that there was also an attractive young man in the castle. One likely to inherit all the wealth, and it was very possible that the beautiful Therese had marked him for her own and regarded any other young female as an intruder.

Eve told them, "I'm very impressed by the chateau."

Maria Langlais sighed. "There are times when one would wish to be free of it and the responsibility that goes with it. But that is not possible. My husband takes his position very seriously."

The Count's keen eyes held an amused gleam. "Miss Lewis does not want to bear about our problems before she has even settled into her own room. I suggest you take her up to the crimson room, Therese. Her bags will be up there by now."

Therese nodded. "Very well," she said coldly.

The Count told Eve, "It will be only a short time before we all assemble for dinner. Leonard will be on hand to greet you then. I'm sure you must be tired after your long journey."

"I actually feel very well," she said.

The Count turned to his wife and said, "Our guest received the cameo we sent her. But she had a rather odd experience in connection with it. It fell on the floor and then a spider bit her. She wasn't sure but-that it emerged from the open locket."

Maria smiled. "I doubt that. I selected the locket for her from my own collection."

Eve felt awkward. "I shouldn't have mentioned it. The spider must have been crawling across the floor when the cameo fell near it. The house is very old. I love the cameo. It's beautiful."

"I'm glad you like it," Maria Langlais said. "It was one of several things I received from a distant cousin. My husband described you to me, and I decided it would be right for you."

"That is so," the Count agreed.

The sad woman with the chalk-white face gave her a searching look. "Now that we've met, I'm certain I made a proper choice."

"I'll wear it at dinner," Eve promised.

"No need," the Count's wife said quietly. "Just so long as you have it with you. You can wear it any time."

Eve smiled, "It's the first cameo I've ever owned."

"We have late dinner here," the Count warned her. "Or at least late by some standards. If you feel you need a snack before nine, let one of the servants know. They can bring you something to your room."

"I doubt if I'll need anything," she said.

Therese had moved to the door and was standing there with a rather disdainful expression on her lovely face. "If you will come with me," she said.

Eve followed the attractive girl with the titian hair back along the shadowed hallway and then up a circular staircase to the second floor of the chateau. There were ornate stained-glass windows along the landing, and these caught her attention. Rather than the familiar religious subjects, these windows picured strange patterns of the Zodiac and abandoned-looking young maidens wearing no covering other than their flowing blond hair. They seemed to be the work of artisans of another period, and Eve determined to question the Count about them.

The forbidding stone walls were decorated at intervals with rich tapestries and an occasional portrait dating back to another century. It was clear to her that the antiques alone must represent a fortune. She could understand why the Count was attached to the fine old estate.

Therese halted before a paneled door and opened it. "This is your room," she said, and led the way in.

Dusk was beginning to settle, and the girl went over to the dresser and lighted two candles in ornate brass candlesticks that were set out there. It gave the room a kind of eerie flickering light. The decor was all in crimson, including the canopy of the wide seventeenth-century bed. The carpet was deep to the step and also in a ruby shade, as were the coverings of the various chairs. The room had a fireplace and closets, and there were two high arched windows with leaded glass.

Eve saw that her luggage had been brought to the room. "It's pleasant," she said, "but so large."

Therese eyed her coldly. "All the rooms in this house are large."

"Have you lived here long?" she asked.

"Long enough," was the brusque reply. And as Eve studied the girl, she noticed for the first time, a faint mark like a strawberry, on her throat. She assumed it was a birthmark.

"The house has a particular interest for me," Eve said. "I like to delve into the mysteries of the past."

The green eyes of the other girl met hers. "There are some mysteries of the past better not disturbed," was her advice. And with that she turned and left the room.

Eve watched after her, wondering what the arrogant Therese had meant. It seemed fairly certain that she was not going to be extended any friendship by the red-haired girl. This could make it awkward. With a sigh she turned to take care of her unpacking. She had no more than ample time to get her things from the suitcases to the dresser and change for dinner.

There was a complete bathroom off her room, and so she was able to take a quick shower. The plumbing and fixtures were modern, suggesting that the Count had taken care of this renovation not too long ago. She decided on a rather elegant green dress that she'd not taken to the seashore. And when she'd put it on and completed combing her hair, she took out the cameo and hung it around her neck. It suited the dress, and she was satisfied with the effect.

She still had fifteen minutes before joining the others downstairs for dinner. Now she began to make a closer study of the room and was deeply impressed by the wood paneling in mahogany, finished in a dark-red varnish and extending three-quarters of the way up the walls. She was standing in the flickering glow of the candles when a soft knock sounded on her door.

Rather timidly she went over and opened it to discover the blond Leonard standing there looking distinguished in dinner jacket and black tie. She gave a small exclamation of delight. “Leonard!”

He came into the room with a faint smile, and she was shocked to see that he looked thinner, almost haggard, and there was a strange, burning gleam in his eyes. “I suppose you find me changed,” he said in a quiet voice.

She stared at him and shook her head. “Not changed, but weary. You show that you have been ill.”

“I have been very ill,” he said in a tense manner.

“Your uncle says you are improving,” she told him. She had never before realized how tall and slim he was. And because of his paleness he seemed even more fragile. His aquiline, handsome face wore a solemn expression.

“I suppose I am,” he agreed. “But I have a long way to go. I couldn’t bear to wait until dinner to see you.”

“I’m glad you came,” she said with a smile.

He took her in his arms and pressed his lips to hers. She thought his embrace much different from those pleasant days in Dinard. Then she’d found his lips warm and caressing. They were something less than that now. His illness had taken a lot from him.

At last he let her go and said, “I’m under the impression you’re shocked by the change in me.”

“I understand,” she said. “I heard about your illness from

your uncle. He explained why you both rushed away."

"That was very difficult for me," the blond man said earnestly. "At Dinard I fell in love with you."

"You mustn't say flattering things to me," she warned him. "I've discovered I'm not the only young girl in the chateau. I've met Therese."

He frowned. "Therese is a vixen!"

"Why do you say that?"

"You'll find out for yourself."

Eve was afraid he was all too right. It seemed plain that Therese regarded her as an intruder and a rival. And Eve didn't want to be either. Changing the subject, she said, "It's a wonderful old castle."

Leonard looked around gloomily. "I have come to regard it as a kind of prison."

"Once you're fully recovered you won't feel that way," she predicted.

He offered her a weary smile. "It will be better now that you are here."

"I hope we can spend a lot of time together as we did at Dinard," she said. "Your uncle hinted you need to rest a good deal."

"I spend most of the day in my apartment," Leonard said, his pale handsome face serious. "I need quiet and complete relaxation."

She sighed. "I hope you have no more attacks."

"Unfortunately the medical world knows very little about the disease," he said. "I would spend a fortune to be certain I was cured. But no one has been able to promise me that."

"You mustn't worry about it. I'll manage very well in the days when you're resting. I'll look forward to when we'll be together and continue my studies of the supernatural."

"It's a consuming interest with you, isn't it?" His eyes searched hers.

She smiled. "It's my field. I hope to continue and win my doctorate in it."

"Yes, of course," he said. "I suppose it's time to join the others."

"It is," she agreed.

As they went out into the shadowed hallway, he said, "Be careful in your conversations with Therese. And don't pay too much attention to anything she says."

Walking at his side, she said, "I have an idea she's terribly jealous of you. That's probably why she resents me. In a way I can understand and not blame her."

He looked grim. "Therese is a fool."

"You're not in love with her?"

"I never have been. My aunt and uncle brought her here with the idea a romance might develop between us. But it didn't work out. Therese has no real understanding of me."

"Does she realize how you feel about her?"

"I doubt it."

"You should make it clear to her."

"She wouldn't listen," the blond man said as they descended the winding stairs.

When they entered the great dining room with its long, white-clothed table and flickering candles in silver candlesticks, the others were gathered by a candle-lit sideboard with glasses in their hands. Count Henri Langlais in black tie bowed to Eve. "What would you like?" he asked.

"A taste of sherry," she suggested, noting that both Therese and the Count's wife had changed to evening gowns. Dinner was clearly a formal affair at the chateau.

The Count gave her a glass of sherry and glanced at Leonard with questioning eyes. "And you, my boy?"

"Nothing, thank you," Leonard said quietly. And in an aside for Eve's benefit, he added, "I drink and eat very little because of my condition."

"I see," she said, taking a sip of her wine. Actually she was badly worried about his changed state. She had not been ready to see such a transformation in him. His physical appearance had altered, and his manner had become solemn and tense. He was a very different person from the charming playboy she had sunned with on the beach at the seaside resort.

After a suitable interlude, the Count summoned them to the dinner table and requested that as the guest of honor, Eve should sit on his right. Therese sat directly across from her, while Leonard sat next to her with Maria facing her husband at the other end of the table. The china and silver were of ancient pattern and probably priceless. A dignified male servant began to serve the first course of fresh fruit.

The Count gave all those at the table a sharp look before they began to eat and said, "I will say the words." And he offered what Eve took to be thanks for the food in words she could not understand. She thought it was Latin, but she understood Latin and could not follow what he said.

When he finished, they began to eat. She felt there was a definite tension at the table and was worried to see that the Count's nephew wasn't making any attempt to touch his portion of fruit. He sat there white-faced and ill-looking, with his hands idle in his lap. She studied the table and wondered what there was about it that struck her as being incongruous. It took her a few minutes to reason it out! The candles were what struck her as odd. They were black!

Normally one expected white candles on a dining table, but all the candles lighting the table were jet black. She wondered why. And now the Count had taken up a silver dish with exactly four thin wafers on it. He passed it to her first with a wise smile.

"There is just one for each of us," he said. "I mean eliminating Leonard, because of his condition. There is a wafer for the rest of us. You must take one and wash it down with the wine. It's a custom of our family."

Even though she had an odd feeling about this rather unusual custom, she took one of the wafers. The Count looked pleased and passed the silver dish to Therese who then gave it with the single remaining wafer to his wife. Eve studied the thin brown wafer before eating it and saw there was the initial L in Old English marked into it. She decided this stood for the family name of Langlais and bit into the waffer. It was strangely tough and had a bitter flavor. She only went on to finish it through politeness. And she was happy to wash away its taste with some of the wine.

The dinner proceeded with a giant roast of beef. Eve glanced at Leonard's well-filled plate and saw that he hadn't touched the main course either. She had the guilty feeling he was terribly ill and making the effort to sit at the table only because she was there.

But when they left the table, he became animated again and invited her for a stroll on the great stone balcony overlooking the chateau gardens and the ocean. "It is best seen at moonlight," was his assurance to her.

The Count smiled at them indulgently. "I know how much you two enjoy being by yourselves," he said. "Please don't hold back on our account."

The Count's wife also gave Eve a smiling nod of approval. It was Therese alone who stared at her with hatred showing in that pretty arrogant face. The redhead was unable to hide her jealousy. And this could lead to unpleasantness.

Yet Eve did not feel like demurring when Leonard took

her gently by the arm and led her out onto the moonlit terrace. It was an enchanted spot, and the grounds and the ocean were enhanced by the silver magic. She and the young man leaned on the stone railing, and his arm went around her as they stared out at the ocean.

She glanced at him half-fearfully and saw that he was absorbed in studying the moonlit water. Quietly, she said, "The way you lose yourself in studying the ocean. It seems to mean something special to you."

"It does," he said, not shifting his gaze. "It offers me peace."

"Peace?"

"I can't try to explain why," he admitted. "Except to say I've gone through great torment, and this is like a balm to me."

Eve's sympathy for the tortured young man was deep and sincere. She said, "I'm terribly worried to find you like this."

Now he turned to her with a wan smile. "I'll improve. I promise."

"You must!"

"Yes, I must," he agreed, his arm tightened around her so that he held her close to him. And he used his other hand under her chin to lift her face towards his. Again he kissed her, and again she wanted to draw back but somehow didn't. As the kiss ended he looked at her solemnly. "I love you, Eve."

"Can you be sure?" There was a tremor in her voice.

"I've had plenty of time to think about it," he insisted. "All the time we've been apart. The long hours I've been forced to rest I've thought only of you! Of your lovely face and what you have come to mean to me!"

His long slim hand caressed her throat gently. And all at once for no good reason she was frightened. He seemed a stranger to her. A menacing stranger. And the horrifying thought crossed her mind that this vague illness he'd suffered might be a mental one. That the man who was protesting his love for her might be insane!

He must have noticed the change in her. "What is it?" he asked.

"Nothing," she said in a small voice and looked away from him.

He touched her arm. "Have I offended you?"

"No," she still stared into the night, avoiding looking at him directly.

"Something is wrong," he persisted, and he gripped her arm. Gripped it so tightly that it brought her severe pain, and she felt she must cry out.

"You're hurting me," she protested, turning to him.

He let her go at once. His handsome face wore a frustrated expression, and there was a tortured burning look in his eyes. Those eyes added to her fear. Surely they held the glitter of madness.

"We're not managing very well, are we?" he said in a voice taut with unhappiness.

"I'm sorry," she said. "It's all strange to me here. And though I knew you had been ill, I didn't expect the illness would make such a change in you."

He stared at her. "Do I disgust you?"

"No," she protested. "You mustn't think that!"

His handsome face showed strain. "Excuse me," he said. And he wheeled away and rushed down the terrace steps to vanish in the dark garden.

She was staring after him when she heard footsteps on the terrace and turned to see the Count. He said, "I must warn you of a danger with Leonard."

She looked up at the aristocratic face of the Count now

bathed in moonlight. "What kind of danger?"

He looked uneasy. "My nephew sometimes has severe attacks of pain. It makes him behave in an erratic manner."

"He certainly behaved that way now," she said. "I thought he might try to strangle me."

The white-haired man shook his head. "You allowed your fears to run away with you. I can guarantee he had no such intention. He was stricken with pain, that's all."

"That's all!" she echoed in consternation. "I have never seen such a change in anyone. What is going to happen to him?"

The Count's aristocratic face was grave as his eyes met hers. "I'd say that depends on you."

"Depends on me?"

"Yes."

"I don't follow you, Count Langlais."

"My nephew is in love with you. He has been since your first meeting on the boardwalk at Dinard."

"He is not the same man now. He is too ill to think of romance."

The Count shook his head. "You are wrong. The doctors consider much of his distress to be caused by his tormented nerves. This isolation in the daylight hours is very bad for him. He needs to know that he is loved. That someone cares and will stand by him. The doctors say this could bring him through the crisis. That at least he could bear his misery better. You could do this for him, Eve. You could marry him."

Her eyes widened. "Do you mean it?"

"I'm asking for my nephew's sake. And I ask your forgiveness for any lapse on his part tonight. He is a sick man. Beyond the help of any of us except you."

"It's not fair of you to say such things to me!"

"I'm beyond the point of being fair, Eve," the elderly man said. "Leonard is the last male of our line. All the hope of the Langlais name rests with him. I don't care what I must do to save him."

She touched a hand to her temple. "I don't know what to say. The man I met tonight does not seem to be the Leonard I knew before. He's a stranger to me. I would not have come if I'd known things were going to be this way."

"I had to get you down here," the Count said simply. "You are my last hope."

"I'd like to go to my room," she said, turning away from him. "I'm suddenly very weary."

The Count seemed sympathetic. "Of course you are. That accounts for most of your distress. Given a good night's rest, all this will seem very different to you."

She made no answer to this, but allowed him to guide her across the terrace to the entrance to the hallway. He saw her to the door of her room and said a quiet goodnight. She quickly went inside and slipped the bolt on the door. The candles on the dresser were still burning, and she went across to the mirror and stared at herself.

Her eyes were stained with tears, and she looked frightened. Moving away from the mirror, she sank disconsolately into a nearby easy chair. What did it all mean? Was there any hope for Leonard? Could she regain the warm feeling she once had for him, the feeling that had surely been close to love? And could her love help bring him back to health as the Count insisted?

It troubled her and made her wonder. It seemed unlikely she could adjust to the sick and tortured young man. And yet she had been very fond of him and wanted to help him if she could. She closed her eyes and thought about all that had happened since her arrival. One of the things that had nagged in the back of her mind were the words of grace he had pronounced before dinner. She felt she should have recognized them and yet she couldn't. And now as she sat there alone in the silence of the nearly dark room, a message flashed through her brain. She knew at last the meaning of the incantation Count Henri Lanalais had offered.

It had been the Black Mass!

Chapter Five

At least a portion of the Black Mass! The words came clearly to mind now. She had memorized them from the pages of a textbook, and she had taken a time to recognize them after hearing them in a strange accent from another. Now she knew!

What did it mean? What sort of evil had she stumbled on at the Chateau Langlais? Was the debonair Count a sort of minor Satan presiding over some diabolical scheme? And had he selected her that night in the dungeon tavern under the streets of Paris because she had stood up and proclaimed herself jokingly a servant of the Devil?

She sat taut in the chair as she reviewed all that had happened to her. The odd illness and the meeting with the doctor who had mysteriously vanished after giving her those pills. What had been in those pills? The first meeting with the charming Leonard. And then the shocking desertion on the part of the young man and his uncle followed by the letter of apology. And then had come the cameo with its poisonous spider enclosed, or so she suspected.

Maybe Simon had been right after all. She'd surrendered herself to an evil group in a house of dark happenings. The Count had offered a Black Mass at the start of dinner. And the candles on the table had been black as well. This had struck her as odd, but it would be in keeping with a Black Mass. And the wafers! Those strange wafers with the letter L that she had believed must stand for Langlais. Could the initial not as well have stood for Lucifer? It all fitted perfectly, and she had sat there, innocently being a part of it.

She was sickened by the memory of it. She knew the Count was versed in sorcery, just as she was. But she had supposed it was a hobby with him. She had never dreamed that he might be a practitioner of the evil. She closed her eyes, realizing how utterly exhausted she was. She could make no decisions until she had some rest. Wearily she prepared for bed.

The night passed without event. Her tiredness had acted as a sedative. And when she wakened, the sun was showing through the two arched windows. She got up and took a shower. And she was finishing dressing when a maid brought her a tray with an ample breakfast.

As she finished her coffee, she debated what she should do. She felt less bitter towards the Count now that she was rested. He was a troubled old man faced with the dying-out of his line. It was not to be wondered that he would attempt desperate measures to save the situation.

Still, she felt coming to the Chateau Langlais had been a mistake on her part. She'd not known how changed Leonard was because of his illness. She was still fond of him, but she felt the best thing would be to give him a chance to recover. When he was well, they could discuss their futures. She had been touched by his confession of love for her last night. She'd also been terrified by the sudden transformation that had made him a crouching beast of prey for at least several seconds.

It was true he'd reverted to himself and apologized. That he'd rushed off to hide his shame in the darkness. But she had to be realistic. No amount of regrets could compensate for seeing him in such a weird state. The best thing would be to ask the Count to arrange to get her to the train returning to Paris.

She went downstairs and found him seated alone on the terrace. He lifted his eyes from the book he was reading as she approached, and rose to greet her. "My dear, Eve," he said. "You look so much better after your rest."

"Yes," she said. "I feel better. And I have decided I want to return to Paris."

"When?"

"Today if that is possible."

"So soon?" The old aristocrat looked dismayed.

"Yes," she said resolutely.

"I had hoped you would feel differently."

She gave him a direct look. "Count, I know at least a part of what is going on here, and I don't like it. You are trying to work some kind of evil spell it seems. Last night's dinner was actually a Black Magic feast. It took me a little time to realize the ritual had been neatly disguised, but you went through with it."

The white-haired man in the linen suit and dark cravat looked shamefaced. He waved her to one of the wicker chairs on the terrace. "Please sit down a moment, Miss Lewis, and listen to me."

She noted that in his apology he had turned from calling her Eve to a more formal Miss Lewis. Still feeling rather sorry for him, she sat in the chair he'd indicated.

"I don't think anything you have to say will interest me," she was careful to warn him.

He sat with his hands clenching the arms of his wicker chair. "I'm a foolish old man. I know that now. I shouldn't have tried to fool anyone as familiar with Black Magic as you."

"Please, explain."

"It began with Leonard's illness," he said sadly. "The doctors have not been of much help. The disease he has is rare, and few know much about treating it. All my life I've had a secret respect for the healing claims of the witch doctor and the voodoo expert. I decided to employ my knowledge of black magic to try and help my nephew. Of course it hasn't worked."

"You should have known better."

"I'm desperate," he admitted. "I'm willing to try anything."

"You're trying too hard it seems to me," she said. "Probably time will help cure Leonard as much as anything else."

The old man regarded her thoughtfully. "Those are sensible words, Eve. And I was at least not wrong about one thing. You are the right kind of girl for my nephew. He needs you badly."

"What can I possibly do for him?"

"Remain here for a little longer. See him in the evenings and try to instill some confidence in him. It's what he needs. You can't judge him fairly by his behavior last night. He was extremely on edge about your arriving and this placed him under extra strain. I'm sure you'd find him more like himself tonight."

"Why not let Therese show some interest in him? She's very pretty and clearly in love with him."

"I have a simple answer for that one," the Count said with a gleam in his shrewd eyes. "Leonard doesn't like her, and he'll not have anything to do with her."

"But he does care for me," she said quietly.

"That could be his salvation."

They sat in silence under the warm sun for a few minutes. Then she gave the white-haired man a challenging glance. "If I agree to remain for a few days, will you put aside your Black Magic practices?"

"I had planned to do that in any case," the Count said. But

there was not the usual air of conviction in his remark.

"Very well," she said in a low voice. "I'll try staying on for a day or two."

"You owe it to yourself," he insisted. "We have a wealth of ancient lore here in this single old building."

"The furnishings are wonderful," she said.

He gave her a knowing smile. "You have only seen part of them. The most interesting are in the cellar."

"The cellar?"

The white-haired man nodded significantly. "The torture chamber, if I must be exact. It has strong links with the sorcery of those other days. You must take a look at it."

For some reason she was wary. "Now?"

"What better time?" he asked, rising. "Later you can go through the old diaries and journals in the library. Between it all you'll get enough material so you won't need textbooks when you return to the university."

She still hesitated. "I suppose Leonard won't be joining us until the evening."

"That is correct," his uncle said. "And I'm hoping tonight he'll be much better. Often he takes dinner by himself and comes to us later. It is sometimes the wisest plan. He's still too nervous to enjoy dinner at the table with a group."

"I know so little about his illness," she said.

"In that regard you are like the rest of us," he assured her. "Now if you'll come with me, I'll give you an interesting tour."

She got up slowly. "I have never seen a true torture chamber," she admitted.

"You'll see one now," he promised.

They went inside and he took her along a different corridor. From it there was a door leading to the cellar and a long flight of stone steps. The Count took a flashlight that had been hanging from a hook on the inside of the door and turned it on to flash the beam over the steps to show her the way. "This is a strong light," he said. "It will be all we'll need."

As she descended into the darkness with him, she began to experience small fears. She wondered if she shouldn't have refused the Count's offer. And she began to tremble a little as he took her by the arm and guided her through a maze of passages with earthen floors. She would never be able to find her way back.

"The cellars extend under all of the chateau," he explained in his suave way. "So we have a very large area down here in this black hole. The section we are passing through now was long used for storage of various foodstuffs."

"And today you don't bother putting things down here?" she inquired.

"No," he said. "We use another part of the cellar. Needless to state, the torture chambers were buried deep in a remote area, and I have records to show they were used by my ancestors."

She gave a tiny shiver caused by the dampness and also by his macabre words. "That must have been a very long while ago."

"Not so long," he said dryly. "The journals make reference to it in the early nineteenth century. So you see none of us are removed too far from savagery."

The dank, sour smell of the dark place was choking her. She wished she had never come, or that it would soon be over. At last he halted and showed the beam of the flashlight on a rusty iron door with a latch on it.

"The torture chamber lies within," he said mockingly. Then he lifted the metal latch. The movement of rusty metal against metal made a creaking, scraping sound that jangled her nerves.

"Must we go inside?" she asked as he swung the door open and a whiff of heavier air from the room filled her nostrils.

"If you wish to make a thorough investigation of the past, you must be brave," the Count told her. His grip on her arm was firm. Now he flashed the beam inside the room, and she could see a number of vague, evil-looking shapes of instruments in the shadows. "We'll see things better at close range." And he shoved her ahead of him into the dread room.

She stood there tensely. "Well?"

"For a start there's a full set of equipment here that was designed to make witches talk if such mild methods as scourging or forced feeding of salted food without water didn't work. But then you are familiar with the persecution of witches so you must know the methods."

"I've never dwelt too much on them," she said nervously.

"So much more reason for your being down here. If you would know a subject, study it at first hand." He shifted the flashlight. "On that side of the room we have the thumbscrew, leg vises, the stocks with iron spikes and the like."

"Surely they would be threat enough," she protested.

"They were more than threats," he assured her. "They twisted and tore limbs until the victims cried out to be relieved of the torture. But there were other treatments for the doomed. In the library there are accounts of men having burning sulphur-dipped feathers applied to their armpits and groins, of their being immersed in scalding water with lime added for good measure."

"I have seen enough," she said weakly.

"Before we go, let me show you the strappado," he insisted. "It was commonly used and highly effective. The apparatus is used to hoist the victim from the ground by his wrists and then tying heavy weights to his ankles. The hoist is in this corner." He began moving away from her, leaving her in the awful darkness of the room of horror. She dug her nails into the palms of her hands and felt the sweat form at her temples.

The Count had gone a dozen yards or so away and was showing the flashlight beam in one corner and then another in an effort to find the torture hoist. She was on the point of calling out to him to return and admitting her fear when he suddenly let out a startled shout himself and apparently stumbled. The flashlight beam vanished, and she was left standing there in silence and cold, clammy darkness.

It had all taken place in a matter of seconds. Finding her voice, she shouted, "What has happened?" But there was no reply from the fallen aristocrat.

Eve stood there in the black fetid atmosphere for another few seconds before calling to the Count again. "Where are you?" she shouted. "Are you hurt badly?"

Her words echoed hollowly in the darkness of the torture room. Knowing the dread instruments that lay all around her, she didn't dare move. A false step could send her stumbling against sharp steel spikes or some other horror designed to tear the flesh. She remained there, frozen in her terror and praying that the next moment would bring some reassuring sound from the Count.

And then she heard the moan. It came to her as if from a distance. It was muffled and full of pain. She tried to picture what might have happened, but in the blackness of the torture dungeon it was impossible to do that. Again she blamed herself for being so unwise as to agree to the expedition. But too late for that now.

Very slowly she turned around in what she was sure must be the direction of the rusty iron door. The Count had left it ajar when they'd entered, and if she could only grope her way to it now, she felt she would at least be out of this place of evil.

She edged across the earthen floor, a half-step at a time, her hands stretched out before her, her eyes striving vainly to make out some sign of the doorway. But it had to be a matter of feeling your way. At last her hand touched the flat rusty surface of the metal door, and she knew a glow of hope.

Stumbling out into the corridor, she tried to decide which way they had come. It had been like a puzzle maze, and she had no confidence she could retrace the route. But she had to make a try. The Count was back there badly hurt, and she had to somehow get help. Not to mention her frantic desire to escape from the black depths herself. With one hand on the rough surface of the passageway, she crept along.

But it seemed a hopeless business. She had no idea whether she was heading in the right direction or not, and she couldn't see anything in the almost pitch darkness. She came to a halt and decided her best bet might be to cry out for help. She did, and beyond the echo of her own voice returning mockingly in the cavelike cellar, there was no reply.

She was about to resume her futile attempts to escape the black depths, when she was alerted by the sounds of shuffling footsteps not far away from her. She listened and knew that the footsteps were growing louder as they came towards her. Again she shouted for help fully expecting an answer this time. But there was none!

Still the shuffling footsteps drew nearer. She stood there, frozen with fear. The vision of rescue had now become the threat of menace from some unknown. A little distance from her, she saw a slight glow of light, and then a figure holding a candle aloft appeared in the tunnel ahead. It was the burly chauffeur, Raol!

"Raol!" she called to him. She had been slightly fearful of

the odd, slow-moving servant, but now she welcomed him.

The huge man came hesitantly towards her, a strange expression on the brute face. The tiny eyes fastened on her warily. She guessed that he might be as afraid of her as she was of him.

"Raol, it is the Count," she said hastily, trusting he would understand. "He took a fall when he was showing me the torture room. I'm afraid he's hurt. We must try to help him. The flashlight was lost when he fell, and I don't know what happened."

The burly man eyed her uncertainly and then shuffled on past her in the direction of the torture room. Though she was still afraid of him, she had no choice but to follow. She couldn't face being alone in the darkness again. The big man lumbered through the entrance to the torture chamber. She forced herself to follow him. The flickering candlelight revealed the grotesque and cruel instruments for inflicting pain set out around them. She averted her eyes from these horrors and looked straight at the broad back of the slowly moving Raol.

He suddenly came to a halt and seemed to be staring down at something. Moving close to him she saw what had caught his attention. A trapdoor in the floor had been left open, and it was through this that Count Henri had surely fallen.

"Down there!" she told Raol.

The big man gave her a grim look and then went down on his knees and held the candle in the trapdoor opening so they could see below. There was a groan, and also a stirring in the inky depths.

In a weak voice the Count called up, "Eve, are you there?"

"Yes," she replied, looking over the brim of the opening. "I have brought Raol. Are you badly hurt?"

"I think not. I have twisted my ankle, and I was temporarily stunned. It also seems I have lost my flashlight."

"Are you far down?" she asked, striving to peer into the hidden room.

"No. I believe I can reach up most of the way if Raol will help me."

The burly man thrust the candle into Eve's hand without a word. And then bent down to assist in lifting the injured nobleman up through the opening in the floor. It took only a moment before the shaken Count came into view. He clung to Raol's hand as he gaspingly emerged through the trapdoor.

When he was safely on the floor of the dungeon, he sat for a moment to recover himself. His white hair was ruffled and his clothing dishevelled. He little resembled the usually debonair squire of the chateau.

He eyed her apologetically. "I'm sorry to have put you through this ordeal," he said. "Somebody left this trapdoor open and I didn't know about it."

Eve had forgotten her own fears in the diversion of rescuing the injured Count. She said, "As long as you're not badly hurt."

"My right ankle is paining. It's just a sprain. If Raol will help support me, I'll be able to make my way upstairs. Once the ankle is bathed and bound I should have little trouble from it."

"I can carry the candle," she suggested. "But you'll have to tell me the way."

"Of course," the elderly man said. And glancing at Raol he told him, "If you'll help me to my feet."

The burly man did as he was ordered. The Count clasped his right arm around him for support, and with Eve leading the way, hobbled out of the dungeon with Raol helping him. Their progress was slow. When they came to a division in the passages, the Count told her which one to take. At last they mounted the stone steps and reached the main area of the house.

Maria was there to greet them. When she saw the sad state of her husband, she became greatly concerned. The Count would have no fuss, and with Raol still assisting him, went on up to his own room to treat his ankle. His wife followed.

So Eve found herself alone on the terrace. She was delighted to sit in the warm sunshine after her frightening experience in the dank cellars of the old castle. She had no wish to ever see the revolting torture chamber again. Though she would study the journals in the library that the Count had mentioned. As long as she was at the chateau, it would be stupid of her not to take advantage of this opportunity for research.

She had agreed to remain at least a few days longer. Perhaps the Count was right. Leonard might show himself in a better light on their next meeting. Their brief romance might not seem so hopeless. She fervently hoped this would be the case.

A shadow suddenly cast itself in front of her, and she looked up with alarm to see the lovely arrogant features of Therese. The shapely secretary was wearing a tiny bikini that revealed her tanned, curvaceous body to the fullest. To protect herself from the sun, she wore a cloak in the same orange shade as the bikini. Large sunglasses in white frames hid her eyes. Again Eve noticed the crimson scar on the girl's throat.

Eve smiled up at her. "You appeared so silently you surprised me."

Therese asked, "Were you expecting Leonard?"

"No."

The redhead's lip curled slightly. "You could have a long wait. He often gets confused about the time these days."

The words caused Eve to know chilling fear again. They

seemed a not too veiled allusion to madness! Had she guessed the truth? That the blond man's breakdown was a mental one? Pretending a casualness she didn't feel, she said, "I understand Leonard's illness."

"Do you?" The girl's tone was mocking.

She stared at her with puzzled eyes. What was the cold, self-contained beauty up to? Was she trying to warn her that Leonard was insane, or was she merely showing jealousy of him?

She said, "You hate me for coming here, don't you?"

Therese's smile was bitter. "I find you very naive."

"Why?"

"If you weren't, you'd leave here," was the girl's surprising reply.

Eve said, "Apart from Leonard the chateau has real interest for me. I like his uncle and aunt, and I'm anxious to learn more about the history of the building."

"You may learn more than you wish!"

Eve stood up facing the other girl. "You keep sneering and making sinister suggestions. Why don't you talk to me in a sensible way?"

"You wouldn't listen if I did," was the girl's parting shot as she left her to go into the chateau.

Eve felt sorry for the attractive girl, but thought she was being foolighly possessive of Leonard, who had clearly stated that he didn't care for her. It had been obvious this was true in his attitude towards her at the dinner table the previous night. Most of the time he'd carefully avoided looking at her or talking to her.

Eve strolled over to the railing to stare down at the flower gardens with their intricate patterns of every hue in the rainbow. She was still standing there when the Count's wife came out to join her.

The pleasant matronly woman appeared troubled. "I have had a bad session with Henri," she complained. "He didn't want to rest his ankle at all. But I persuaded him to remain in bed for the afternoon. I've also called the doctor, and he can take a few minutes with Leonard at the same time."

"Does the ankle seem badly swollen?"

"Yes. I worry that it might be broken. But Henri insists not. He can be a very stubborn man."

"I understand," Eve said.

"And we have a party planned in your welcome tomorrow night," Maria worried. "It is too late to cancel it. I only hope that Henri will be able to take his place as host."

"I'm sorry you went to such trouble."

A faint smile showed on the white face of the older woman. "But we wanted to do it," she said. "We are anxious that you should meet some of our friends and neighbors."

"I would like to spend some time in the village," Eve explained. "I read something about a woman who was accused of being a vampire. She was later murdered. The Count promised to tell me the details since it all happened in Langlais. But he hasn't had the opportunity yet."

A strange, haunted look had come to Maria's face. "I would not mention that incident to anyone," she warned her. "The people of the village are a sickeningly superstitious lot. You could end being accused of having the evil eye yourself."

She showed amazement. "I had no idea."

"This is a small, isolated part of the world, my dear," the older woman said. "You must remember that. My husband does not allow his interest in the supernatural to become widely known. It is a hobby of which only a few friends are aware."

"I see," she said.

"Now you must excuse me," Maria smiled. "There are

many things still to get ready for our party tomorrow evening."

Eve remained on the terrace alone for some time before going to her room. She had been puzzled by the uneasiness Maria had shown at the mention of the vampire woman and the facts of her murder. There were many things about the people living at the chateau she did not fully understand.

The Count's attempts to invoke black magic to restore Leonard's health might be an act of desperation on the old man's part, but certainly was not in character. She wished there was some easy way of leaving the chateau. She needed to get away from the eerie atmosphere of the place and try to think it all out.

But she vividly remembered that iron fence being padlocked behind their car. And the Count had let her know a high fence charged with electricity guarded the estate from the outside world. The same fence also made prisoners of anyone like her who happened to be inside it. She could not escape without the Count's approval and assistance. And she was sure he would give neither.

She didn't dare dwell too much on this. She couldn't afford to panic. And brooding fear of what might be going on around her while she remained a virtual prisoner could only lead to hysteria. Better not to worry about the possibility of Leonard being insane and the Count's urgent desire that she marry his nephew. Weary, she sought the solace of the crimson canopied bed and slept for a good part of the afternoon. She awoke feeling refreshed. After a shower, she changed into a suitable gown for dinner and went downstairs. She was just in time to come upon Maria standing in the shadowed entrance hall with a stoutish man carrying a small black bag. Eve at once surmised this to be the doctor.

As the two heard her coming down the stairs, they turned to look her way. She halted with a gasp. For the man with the black bag was the same Dr. Devereaux who had so mysteriously vanished at Dinard!

Chapter Six

The doctor and Maria Langlais exchanged glances. Then the gray-haired woman came to the foot of the stairs and said, "Mademoiselle Lewis, I would like to have you meet the doctor, who is also one of our oldest friends in the village."

Eve continued down to the hall, and with a faint smile for the doctor said, "I believe we have met somewhat briefly before."

Maria's white face showed interest. "Really?"

"Yes," Eve said. "At Dinard, Doctor. Surely you remember."

The stout man's broad face had turned a brick red. "I regret that I do not, Mademoiselle."

"But I have the empty pill bottle upstairs with your name on it, Dr. Devereaux."

Again Maria and the Doctor exchanged significant glances. And Maria was quick to say, "But this is not Dr. Devereaux. It is Dr. Jardin."

Eve stared at them in astonishment. She told the stout man with the bag, "I can't be mistaken. You look exactly like Dr. Devereaux."

The broad face showed a weak, apologetic smile. "I'm sorry. But you are confused. I am not your Dr. Devereaux, and I have never visited Dinard."

She did not know what to say. For some reason best known to himself, the doctor wanted to deny his presence at the seaside resort. She could only content herself with,

"There is a remarkable resemblance."

Maria was quick to pick up this cue. "That often happens. And I'm sure Dr. Jardin will not mind your mistaking him for someone else. I make the same sort of error all the time with other people."

The doctor nodded. "I have an ordinary face, Mademoiselle. Your mistake is understandable." He bowed to her, and turning to Maria said, "If Henri will not try to use the ankle too much, he will recover quickly."

"Thank you," the Count's wife said. "And about Leonard?"

The doctor's brow wrinkled. "Ah, that is another matter. I am awaiting word from Paris about some new drugs that may help him. But I fear the only thing we can truly count on is the sort of regression he had before."

"Is this likely?" the pale woman asked.

"A good question," Dr. Jardin said. "I hesitate to make any firm predictions."

Maria sighed. "Thank you, Doctor. You will be attending the party tomorrow night, of course."

"I shall certainly come if my professional duties do not interfere," he promised. And with another bow he left.

Maria escorted Eve into the living room. She had the impression the older woman was anxious to make her feel at ease. And she felt anything but that way. The incident of the doctor had been another disquieting factor. She was positive this was the same man she'd known as Dr. Devereaux, but no one was going to admit it.

Maria invited her to sit down and indicated the crystal chandelier and the ornate furnishings of the vast living room. "We have a kind of minor museum in this room," she said proudly. "My husband will not let any of the valuable old pieces be removed or sold."

"It is a beautiful room," Eve said, glancing from the fine pieces of furniture to the rich paintings in gilt frames that hung on the walls. As she studied the various portraits, she noticed a pen sketch in a black frame. It was of medium size and caught her attention for a particular reason. She got up and went over to inspect it. "This drawing bears a remarkable likeness to Leonard," she exclaimed.

Maria nodded. "Yes. And to make it more of a coincidence, the man who sat for that drawing was also a Leonard Langlais. He lived here a century ago."

Eve continued to stare at the sketch. "In so many details their faces are the same. Does Leonard know about this?"

"Yes, it amuses him," Maria said, with one of her sad smiles. "He always insists that his ancestor was a much more handsome man."

Eve frowned at the sketch of the serious face. "Judging by this I see little difference between them." She turned to the older woman. "I must soon make a study of some of the family journals. The Count claims there are many in the study and has offered me access to them."

Maria nodded. "Henri has had many of them bound in leather. There is a full shelf of the volumes. He'll be glad to show them to you once he is up and around."

"There is no hurry."

Count Henri Langlais made his usual appearance at dinner. He leaned heavily on a cane, but he walked without much limp. Therese sat in her usual place with downcast eyes and saying little, while Leonard did not join them at all.

Maria commented on this. "I assume Leonard is dining in his apartment," she said.

"Yes," the Count nodded. "I expect we'll see him shortly." Turning to Eve, he added, "Tomorrow we shall be dining earlier. We have about thirty guests invited here later.

We shall have a musicale and end the evening with a light buffet."

"It is good of you to have the party," she said. "If your ankle bothers you, there's no reason why you shouldn't cancel it."

"Not at all," the Count said firmly. "Though I am glad we didn't decide on an evening of dancing. My ankle wouldn't be equal to that. As it is, I can seat myself somewhere in the living room and hold court."

"Leonard will see that your guests are looked after well," the Count's wife said. "It is important that he conserve himself for the party on that account."

The Count gave his attention to the sullen, lovely Therese. "I have no doubt you will treat us with a new gown for the occasion," he said.

"I may not choose to attend," Therese said quietly.

The Count looked concerned. "Come, that is no way to talk. We must do our guest honor."

Eve was only too well aware that Therese had little interest in taking part in an affair to honor her. She was sorry that the Count had planned the evening. She would have much preferred avoiding this kind of social event.

When dinner ended, she joined the others in a liqueur in the big living room. And while she was standing there talking with the Count, the familiar figure of Leonard appeared to stand framed in the doorway. The handsome blond man was dressed in white flannels with a pale blue cravat and matching handkerchief in his jacket pocket. He looked much more like the man she'd known in Dinard than he had the previous evening.

The Count smiled at her. "Go to him," he advised her. "I am returning upstairs in a few minutes."

Eve quickly excused herself and hurried across the room

where Leonard still stood. She smiled at him and said, "You seem so much better tonight."

He took her hand, and she was mildly surprised to find he wore white gloves. Seeing her expression of astonishment, he said, "I have a circulation problem. Even on the hottest nights my hands become cold. I'm wearing these on the doctor's advice."

"Yes, I met him today."

"Let's not waste the evening standing here," he said, with a glance at the others gathered at the far end of the living room. "We have so much to talk about."

"We have," she agreed.

He led her out of the house and stood for a moment on the terrace. The light was blurred as dusk lingered before turning to night. He still held her hand in his. It was like the old days at Dinard. Eve was thankful she hadn't impulsively left. Leonard was coming back to himself, and they still might find happiness together.

"Have you been down to the beach yet?" The handsome man with the wavy blond hair asked her.

"No."

"You must go. The water isn't too cold, and the beach itself is excellent," Leonard told her with a smile. "Better than that at Dinard and much more private."

"Perhaps I'll go tomorrow," she said. "I dislike going alone. If Therese wasn't in such a sullen temper, I'd invite her along."

"She can be difficult," he acknowledged. "I'll show you the way before it gets dark. And we can take a short walk along the cliffs."

"Have we time?"

"It's not far," he said, leading her down the steps to the garden.

Eve was actually surprised at how direct the path to the beach was. Rather than go all the way down, he took her for a stroll along the cliffs. He seemed to take a keen enjoyment in this, and even though it was now nearly dark, he would stop every so often and stare out across the water.

"What can you possibly see in this light?" she demanded jokingly.

He turned to her with a wise smile. "I happen to have very sharp sight. Especially for distances. I can see things invisible to your eyes."

She stared at him. "That sounds ghostlike."

The handsome face was sad. "I didn't mean it to. But then, aren't you fascinated by the supernatural?"

"At a reasonable distance," she laughed.

"I'll keep that in mind," he said.

They walked on, and then he led her down a steep path to the beach itself. Finding a sheltered spot among the rocks, they sat side by side. He told her, "This is one of my favorite places. I've been coming here a long while."

She nestled close to him, and his arm went around her. It was exactly as it had been at Dinard. She murmured, "It's so wonderful to have you like your old self again."

"I'm sorry to be so difficult," he said. "But I am trying to fight my way back to normal health."

"I keep telling myself that."

"I rested even more than usual today," he went on. "I must be at my best for your party tomorrow night. I'll help with the guests, especially if my uncle's ankle is still bothering him."

Eve studied his handsome profile with dreamy eyes. "Would you believe that I thought of trying to leave here? I might have run away if I hadn't known the estate is shut off by that electric fence and locked gates."

"I suppose my illness frightened you," he said. "I have sudden bouts of pain." He stared out at the ocean.

"I know. And I didn't mean to become panicky."

Leonard gave her a serious look. "All that I ask is that I recover enough to have you become my wife."

And he took her in his arms and kissed her gently. Even though it was not quite the same as it had been at Dinard, she couldn't believe the arms that held her belonged to a madman. She hated herself for ever having doubted him so.

When he let her go, she said, "It's bound to be all right."

"Yes," he said quietly.

They sat there with the roll of the ocean in their ears and talked of many things. She told him about seeing the pen sketch of the Leonard Langlais of long ago, and he seemed amused. And she gave him a description of her terror in the dungeon beneath the old castle.

He frowned. "My uncle shouldn't have taken you down there."

"He meant well."

"Still, it was foolish of him," the blond man complained. "And I shall tell him so."

She frowned. "And then there was a misunderstanding about the doctor when he came." And she explained about the embarrassment of the meeting.

The blond man in the white flannel suit heard her out. Then he said, "I'm inclined to believe you must have made a mistake."

"But it doesn't seem possible."

"Dr. Jardin is not the type of man to deny the truth. And he rarely leaves the village. In fact I know that he was here when my uncle and I were in Dinard. At the moment I was taken ill my uncle's first thought was to rush me back here to Dr. Jardin."

"Could two men look so much alike? Two doctors?"

"Why not? As Dr. Jardin admitted, he is a rather common middle-aged type. I'm sure he and your Dr. Devereaux only seemed exactly alike in your memory. If you saw them together, there would be a difference. One might be slightly taller or thinner than the other, and there could be a mole on the side of one face or a birthmark on the cheek of the other."

"Perhaps so," Eve said, reluctantly allowing him to convince her. And then, as it came to mind, she added, "Therese has a strange red spot on her neck."

"A birthmark," Leonard said. "I once heard her discussing it with my aunt."

"It is time to go back," she smiled at him. "I know you only have the nights. But I don't want your family to get a bad impression of me. And I do begin to feel tired."

He helped her to her feet. "You need your rest for the party."

"What will you do the balance of the night?"

He smiled. "I wander a good deal. Sometimes take strolls in the village. Then I go back to my apartment in the west wing and read."

"I have never seen your part of the castle."

"When we are married, you'll live there," he promised.

They strolled back to the gardens. The night was dark without any sign of a moon. Eve mentioned this to him. "I find it scary," was her comment.

"I have learned to like the darkness," he said. "Of course it has been necessary."

"We were so happy at Dinard in the sun," she said in a mournful tone. "I hope you will get better."

They were at the entrance to the castle now. Leonard nodded. "With you here to give me courage, I'm sure I will."

He saw her to the door of her room, and they kissed goodnight. Inside she bolted the door as usual and felt the evening had been a success. If the Count's nephew continued to improve as he had in the past twenty-four hours, she felt certain he would be able to risk the sunlight again. With this comforting thought she began to prepare for bed by the flickering candlelight.

But on this night her dreams of terror were destined to return. It must have been because of her frightening ordeal in the torture chamber. At any rate, she wakened in the middle of the night to what seemed like a distant feminine scream. She sat up in bed, not knowing whether she'd actually heard the cry or if she'd dreamed it. Still curious, she rose and went over to the nearest of the windows and opened it a little. She could see no sign of anyone.

After moments of uncertainty, she returned to bed and fell asleep. And then the nightmares crowded in on her. She was on the terrace in the darkness, and a giant bat emerged from the shadows and came to attack her. She cried out her terror and fought the persistent, sickly softness of the revolting thing as it hovered around her head. Then she felt its teeth sink into her throat, and in the moment of searing pain she fainted.

She drifted in a strange state not quite conscious, and Therese was standing at the foot of her bed with an arrogant smile on her face. The redhead wore a flowing white nightgown of some transparent material. And at her side stood the handsome Leonard. Eve stared at the two in disbelief, and then she saw the blood trickling down from that red mark on the neck of Therese! Fresh blood running down in two tiny streaks!

The horror of it brought her out of her coma, and she cried out and came awake. Sitting up, she saw there was no one there. She was completely alone in the shadowed room. But the picture of Therese and the blond man had been so vivid, she found it hard to accept it had been a nightmare. She sat propped against her pillows, staring into the darkness and wondering what it had meant. She was still sitting that way as dawn approached and her eyes drooped shut.

After she'd had breakfast, she donned her bathing suit and terrycloth dress and went downstairs. When she reached the terrace, she saw the Count standing in the driveway talking gravely to someone in a dark sedan. While she hesitated there watching him, the lovely Therese came up beside her.

"The Count is discussing last night with the authorities," she informed Eve.

Eve turned to her. "What happened last night?"

"One of our servant girls was mysteriously attacked," Therese said with a wise expression. "It has happened before, but not lately."

Remembering the scream she was certain she'd heard, she asked, "Where did it happen?"

"In the gardens not far from here."

That fitted in with her memory of the forlorn cry. She said, "Was the girl badly hurt?"

"She's like the others who've had the same experience. She seems all right except for a weird mark on her throat, and she doesn't remember anything."

"That sounds like a description of the victims of the vampire woman. But she was murdered three years ago."

Therese shrugged. "These attacks on the village girls have never ceased."

"That's odd," Eve said.

"Isn't it," the redhead said, a mocking light in her lovely eyes. And Eve couldn't take her eyes from the girl's slender throat and that red mark, which in the morning light seemed more livid than ever. The car drove away, and Count Henri

Langlais came limping up the steps to join them.

Leaning on his cane, he said, "Why is it that the stupid authorities always come to pester me when there has been a crime committed in the village. I cannot be responsible for all my employees. Now they want to take Raol in for questioning."

"Because of what happened to the girl last night?" Eve asked.

He frowned. "You've heard about it."

"Yes."

"Most unfortunate. But I say someone in the village is to blame. I'm sure it wasn't Raol."

She looked at the old man's angry face. "It reminds me of the vampire case."

"Really?" the Count's tone was icy. "I'm sorry I haven't time to discuss such theories now. You will excuse me." He bowed and went on into the house.

Eve glanced at Therese and saw the jeering smile on the redhead's face. She knew it was useless to invite her along to the beach. So using the path Leonard had shown her, she went alone. The beach was sandy and wide, and best of all, she had it to herself.

Stretched out in the sun, she considered the events of the night. And it seemed to her there must be a vampire still at large in the village of Langlais. It was the only thing to explain the continuing attacks. The old woman might not have been a vampire at all. The true vampire could have murdered her after casting the suspicion her way. And he might still be at large to continue his fiendish attacks on the innocent.

It was an unsettling thought, and it led to others. Who, better than the Count, could approach such a problem in this tiny village? And why was he so loath to discuss the case? There was no question that he was an expert in the field of black magic, and he'd even admitted to holding a kind of Black Mass at the dinner table the night of her arrival in the hope of restoring Leonard to health. Why wasn't the Count taking a leading part in trying to track down this perpetrator of the mysterious assaults?

Why, indeed, unless he knew that someone among his circle of friends or one of his employees was guilty? Or could he actually be guilty himself? It was a frightening thought, but such things did happen. Leading figures in a town or city became involved in dark practices and for long periods were never even looked on as suspects. Count Henri Langlais could be such a person.

The idea excited her, and she intended to discuss it with Leonard when she saw him in the evening. If only the Count's handsome nephew were not fighting his dread illness, things would be a lot simpler. They would be able to work together so much better. But the prospects were encouraging. He was improving.

She spent the entire morning at the beach, and in the afternoon she went to the Count's study and began to check the various volumes having to do with the history of the Langlais family, and also those volumes that dealt in witchcraft and other aspects of the black arts. Her fascination with them absorbed all her attention. She sat in the dusty study poring through the rare titles.

There were some modern books on the subject as well, and one contained a reference to the Black Mass that caught her attention, "The Black Mass is still with us," she read. "Even in this modern age there are said to be active groups of Satanists in the most exalted social circles of the Western world. In London, New York and Paris, there are known to exist active groups devoted to Lucifer. And in the smaller provincial towns of both France and England, there are cults of Devil-worshippers. They have their secret signs, their own meeting places, and a strict code of secrecy as to the identity of their members. At their rituals, black is the hallowed color. Black candles and black wines are only the symbols of the potent evil their allegiance brings about. Many prominent figures have at various times been suspected of links with this mafia of the supernatural."

She closed the book with a puzzled expression on her pretty face. And she was still sitting there when Maria entered the study. "I have been looking for you," she said. "I wanted to tell you something about the party tonight."

"Oh, yes," she said, rising.

The pale face of the older woman showed a strange eagerness. "The Count and I are anticipating it. And we are holding it in a section of the chateau we usually keep shut off. There is an ancient chapel there stripped of much of its fine trappings but still most interesting. It is a large room and will allow our guests to move about freely. Leonard will escort you there when he arrives."

"What time will the party begin?"

"At dusk. So Leonard may play his full part in it," she said. And then with a hesitant smile, she asked, "What do you plan to wear, my dear?"

"Is it to be a formal affair?"

"Yes. The Count likes to dress in the evenings."

"I have several suitable things with me," Eve said. "You have seen the green gown. And there is my black one."

Maria's pale face brightened. "The black one, by all means. I'm sure it is in excellent taste."

Eve gave the matter little thought. She put on the black gown and used the cameo as a decoration again since it suited the dress. But when she sat down at the dinner table, she was surprised to see that both Therese and Maria were wearing black gowns as well. She wondered if they wouldn't present too somber an appearance in their united front.

Count Henri Langlais had put aside his cane, though he still limped slightly. "I'll not present myself to my guests appearing to be a cripple," he announced.

Leonard arrived shortly after dinner wearing a black tie and dark jacket. He gave Eve an admiring glance and said, "I've never seen that gown before."

"I hope you like it."

"Exactly right for you and the occasion," was his pleased comment. Then he led her down a long dark corridor to a part of the house she'd never been to before. At the end there was an open door leading to another shadowed corridor, and at the end of it, double doors led directly into the ancient chapel.

The great room with its vaulted ceilings was dimly lighted, and she saw that some guests had already arrived. The majority of them seemed to be men in formal dress, but there were a few women of various ages mixed in the group. The Count and Maria were receiving. And she saw that there was a side entrance to the chapel leading from the garden. The arriving guests were using this entrance.

"What do you make of it?" Leonard asked her.

She glanced around at the richly paneled room with its altar and fine tiled floor. "It's a most unusual setting for a party," she said.

"My uncle enjoys the unusual," Leonard assured her. "Now you must join the reception line with me since the affair is in your honor."

"Must I?" she asked, knowing that she would have to agree.

They took their places beside the Count and Maria. Of course Leonard knew everyone and introduced her to them. Many of the names were lost to her, but she had a vague impression of a host of smiling faces. She hoped that she would recognize them when she met them again, but doubted it.

One person she did not miss was the stout Dr. Jardin. He came down the line in company with a surprisingly young and beautiful dark girl whom he introduced as his wife. Eve still could not help wondering if he were not the Dr. Devereaux who had with his pills so successfully brought an end to her illness at Dinard.

As others were introduced, she began to realize that most of the men were of the Count's age, while the women, with the exception of Maria and a few others, were all rather young and mostly attractive. And black was the prevailing color of their gowns, though there were one or two velvet crimsons. She was considering this and barely paying attention to what was going on.

Her eyes lifted to the walls where the candles were flickering, and she saw that they were black. Her heart began to pound more rapidly. Had the Count tricked her into taking part in another of his black magic rituals? Instinctively she glanced towards the table with the wines and buffet, and she saw that while the cloths covering the long sweep of tables were white, the plates were black and gold. And the wine being poured into the glasses was jet black!

She gave Leonard a frightened look, anxious to point this out to him, but he was in conversation with a dignified gray-haired man with piercing eyes and hollow cheeks. Turning to her right, she saw the Count and Maria were talking to another couple. Panic grew in her like a sudden blaze of fire. Glancing across the room, she saw Therese standing with the stout Dr. Jardin and his wife. And she had the immediate impression that the three of them were talking about her.

She stood there transfixed, and then realized that Leonard

had touched her arm gently. "Eve, I'd like you to meet Father Boulanger," he said. "For many years he was our parish priest."

Numbly, Eve turned to greet the priest, and then her eyes widened. For standing smiling at her in the shabby black cassock of a priest was the parchment-faced old man from the train compartment! The ruined, gaunt face showed a smile, and the gaping black mouth revealed foul yellow stubs of teeth. Eve thought she would faint as memories of the train compartment and that day in the weird drugstore surged back to haunt her. This was the identical ghostly old man!

Chapter Seven

The old man in the clerical collar and cassock continued to smile at her and extended a thin, clawlike hand for her to shake. Hardly knowing what she was doing, she shook hands with him. The deep-sunk eyes with their yellow coating studied her. The supposed Father Boulanger looked more like a dried-up corpse than a human being.

In a harsh voice the old man said, "What a pleasure to at last meet you, Mademoiselle. The Count has said so many fine things concerning you."

"Thank you," she managed in a choked tone.

"You and this young man make a handsome couple," Father Boulanger said with a knowing cackle. "I vow it will not be long before the banns are given for you." And he moved on to greet the Count.

Eve closed her eyes and wavered slightly. In a low voice she told Leonard, "Please take me out to the garden. I think I'm going to faint!"

"Eve!" His tone was urgent as he took her arm.

She did not look to left or right as he swiftly led her from the shadowed chapel out into the near darkness of the garden. When they were a distance beyond the cars drawn up before the chapel entrance, she halted and gazed up at him in terror.

"I've seen that old man before!"

Leonard's handsome face showed a frown. "Eve! You're being silly! This is happening too much! First it was the doctor and now poor old Father Boulanger! Where could you possibly have met him?"

"In the train on my way to Dinard," she said in a frantic tone. "And then later in a drugstore. He gave me an injection of some drug!"

"Wait a minute!" the young man said in a shocked voice. "You're really way off. Your imagination is much too vivid, and you're allowing it to run wild!"

"I'm telling you the truth!" she insisted.

"Father Boulanger has not been out of this village in years," Leonard said in a troubled voice. "He had some trouble with his bishop and was retired about three years ago. He's lived a frugal, hermit existence since. My uncle is one of his few friends."

"It had to be him!" she persisted.

"Just as Dr. Jardin had to be Dr. Devereaux," he reminded her. "There are people who look alike and you must accept that. You're in some kind of near hysterical state or you wouldn't make these accusations."

"No wonder," she said, close to tears. "Do you think I'm so stupid as not to know what is going on in there? That the so-called party for me in that chapel is nothing more than the gathering of a Satanist society."

Leonard stood there wordless, his handsome face showing surprise. "That's a serious accusation."

"I know I'm right," she said. "You and your uncle seem to forget I have made a study of such things."

"Very well," he said. "You are right. This is a meeting of a Black Magic group, but it is also a party for you. My uncle arranged it as a surprise. This society is devoted to research in the field just as my uncle is. They are not joined to do evil but to examine its nature."

Eve was still unconvinced. "So you say! There is something very strange about all those people. They're not quite normal. The entire atmosphere in there is poisoned by what they are and what they do."

He gave her a grim smile. "If I'm not wrong, the first time my uncle met you was at a drunken orgy, and you caught his attention by leaping on a table and proclaiming yourself a high-priestess devoted to Satan."

"It was a students' party not an orgy," she replied bitterly. "And I said what I did as a joke. Those people in there are deadly serious in their evil."

"In their research," he corrected her. "They are students of the macabre just like you. They are not enrolled in any college, but group together to exchange information and share their mutual interest."

"Your uncle should have explained this to me," she said, still filled with doubt.

"He intended to later in the evening," Leonard assured her.

"I can't go back there," she said unhappily. "I'm too upset."

"You needn't, if you don't want to," Leonard said. "The musicale has begun, and they probably won't miss us in any case. I'm worried about you and these strange delusions you harbor. You seem to be looking for evil in all around you."

Eve sighed. "I'm sorry. I probably am overwrought. I didn't sleep well last night. And then I heard about that poor girl being attacked on the grounds." She gazed earnestly into his handsome face. "It sounded like a vampire's attack. One of these people in there may be quietly mad and believe himself to be a vampire. They could be making the attacks against the village girls. Have you thought of that?"

The blond man frowned. "I think those girls often make up stories of being attacked to get attention."

"And make marks on their throats?"

"Even that is possible with hysterical females," he said

very sternly. "And I don't want to count you among them. You must close your ears to this village gossip."

Eve was surprised by his vehemence. "You sound very sure."

"I'm trying to protect you from your own taut nerves," he said more gently and took her in his arms.

They were still locked in an embrace when she heard the footstep behind her. Instinctively she pulled herself away from him and turned to see who the intruder was. It was Therese!

Leonard stepped forward angrily. "How dare you spy on us?"

Therese paid no attention to him, but turned to her with her lovely face distorted by anger and contempt. "You little fool!" she cried and then swept back towards the chapel entrance.

They waited until the chapel door was opened and then heard a brief snatch of harpsichord music. Then the door closed again as the titian-haired girl went inside. Leonard had been glaring in the direction of the door, and now he sighed and turned to her.

"That girl has gone too far," he said tensely. "I'll speak to my uncle after the party tonight. She must be put in her place."

"I'm the one who should leave," she said. "I'm the intruder."

"Don't talk that way, Eve," he said sharply. "I'm in love with you. I want to marry you."

She stared at him. "You must have given her some encouragement before I came along?"

"I treated her in a friendly manner as I would anyone in the house," he protested. "She has abused my friendship."

"I don't feel like talking about it now," she said, closing

her eyes. "I have a splitting headache. I'm going to my room. You'd best return to the party and make apologies for me."

The young man looked forlorn. "I don't want to go without you."

"Please do. It will look less strange. Say that I was suddenly taken ill. And it is true. My head is splitting!"

"I could speak to Dr. Jardin," he suggested. "No doubt he could give you something."

"Thank you, no," she said. "Goodnight, Leonard."

They kissed briefly, and she went up to the main entrance door of the chateau and inside. Her head continued to throb long after she'd reached her own room and prepared for bed.

She lay awake in the dark room, and later heard the cars of the party guests drive off. She was haunted by the grotesquely familiar face of the old man who was supposedly Father Boulanger. She wanted to believe what Leonard had told her but it was difficult. All of them were part of the secret society devoted to a study of Satanism—the doctor, the old priest, Maria, Therese and the Count. Were they all working together in some subtle fashion to convert her?

She had been wrong to accept the Count's friendship so quickly. Simon had been right in that. Yet if Leonard's version of things was true, the group that had gathered in the chapel were no more than old friends interested in the folklore and legend of the rugged Brittany coast. Until she had evidence to the contrary, she supposed she should believe what Leonard said. He loved her and did all he could to protect her in spite of his serious illness.

But Therese had called her a fool. And there must be some meaning behind her words. If there was anything of a bizarre nature being plotted against her, Eve was sure the red-haired girl had knowledge of it. Perhaps if Therese became angry enough, she would burst out with whatever secret information she had. It was a distinct possibility.

She had no idea when sleep came to her, but she was wakened by a knocking on her door. Sitting up in bed, she saw that it was morning and the sun was shining.

Calling out, she asked, "Who is it?"

"Count Langlais," came in the elderly man's familiar voice. "May I speak with you a moment?"

"Yes," she said. Quickly getting out of bed, she put on her robe and slippers and went to open the door.

The white-haired man looked grave. "May I step inside?"

"Please do."

He avoided her eyes. "I have unhappy news," he said. "Therese is dead."

"Therese! Dead!" she echoed him.

"Yes. A suicide. She threw herself from the cliffs. One of our workers found her broken body on the rocks below this morning. She must have done it after the party last night."

Eve was stunned. "I can't believe it!"

"She was a strange girl," the Count said, his handsome aquiline face shadowed. "I suspect she was madly in love with Leonard and crazily jealous of him."

"Of course that's true!"

The Count stared at the crimson carpet. "I worried that it might end in tragedy as my nephew had no interest in her. But I had hoped to avoid anything like this."

"Leonard must be told," she said.

"He knows about it."

She stared at him. "How?"

"I took the liberty of taking the word to him myself," the elderly man said. "I never intrude in his apartment at this hour of the day, but I made an exception."

"What was his reaction?"

"He is upset, of course. But he is not in any way to blame.

None of us are. The girl had a penchant for self-destruction."

Eve was only now beginning to realize what the suicide of Therese meant. The girl was silenced forever. Anything she might have learned from her was lost now. And she couldn't help wondering if the spur that had driven Therese to suicide hadn't been the realization that she'd lost Leonard. The discovery of her in his arms must have made that seem final.

She tried to think of something to say. All she could manage was, "Will the funeral be held from here?"

"Very quietly. She'll be buried in our private cemetery. A closed casket because of the condition of the corpse. Just a few friends in attendance with Father Boulanger to conduct the service."

"I see," Eve said quietly. "I should be there."

"I'd prefer that you wouldn't," the Count said. "I discussed this with my nephew, and he was of the same opinion. You've been under too much strain as it is. You must take care of yourself. Remember you came here for a holiday."

She did not feel in a mood to argue about it. "Whatever you think," she said quietly.

The Count moved towards the door. "I wanted you to know. Tonight you'll have plenty of time to discuss it with Leonard. I'm sure he'll make you look at it in a philosophical manner. We must learn to be sensible even in the face of death." And with this said the Count left her.

She dressed slowly and was able to eat little breakfast. She went downstairs and sat alone on the terrace. A mood of depression seemed to have settled over the chateau despite the sunny day. She did not dare to guess where the body of Therese might be and if it would be brought to the castle to rest overnight. Her first reaction was to feel heartbroken for the unhappy girl.

And then she began to have other thoughts. Disturbing

thoughts! She remembered Leonard's anger with the redhead the previous night. His comment that she had forgotten her place and must be taught a lesson. He had mentioned that he would speak to his uncle about her. All innocent enough indignation perhaps, yet suppose he had told his uncle the story. If the Count had any ulterior plot underway that he felt Therese might endanger, how easy it would be for him to murder the girl and claim she had killed herself. The battered body and the closed casket would defy the authorities to prove anything else!

Here in this remote land it was possible! The easiness of it sickened her. And she knew that again she was doing what Leonard had warned her against, allowing her imagination too free a rein. With a sigh she rose from the wicker chair and went into the great mansion. Since she was anxious to get her mind off the tragedy, she decided she would spend the day in research. So she settled down in the study with a number of the Count's books.

The first one she read was a family history. It had been written in a crabbed hand, and the Count had arranged for the voluminous diary to be given a binding like a book. Some sections were in faded brown ink and had almost become impossible to read. Yet she persevered and was well-rewarded with an engrossing account of the Langlais family in another day.

They had known royal favor, and their lands had been bestowed on them by one of the long-ago monarchs of France. As she read on she suddenly came upon a mention of Leonard Langlais. He had become a Count and the family head in the early eighteen-hundreds. From the records, he was a man of learning and had the reputation of being generous to his tenants. But suddenly this fine family man gained a reputation of consorting with a witch, a young and fair woman of the village who was known to be in league with the Devil. And as a consequence, the younger brother of Count Leonard took them in custody and questioned them in the torture chamber of the castle.

Eve became increasingly excited as she flicked over page after page reading the dramatic account. She pictured the framed sketch of the Leonard Langlais who looked so much like the Leonard of today with whom she was in love. And she read on. In the torture chamber, both the maiden and the handsome Count Leonard confessed to doing Satan's work. And so the Count's younger brother had privately burned them both at the stake. The entry in the journal finished with a pious, "God save us from their kind!"

She put the ancient volume aside with a feeling of despair. Was the history of man nothing but a record of superstition, cupidity and violence? She was certain the younger brother of Count Leonard had wanted the estate for himself and so had cleverly cast suspicion on the two. That they confessed in the dread torture chamber was no surprise. She had seen the chamber and its array of ingenious devices.

She had a snack sent in to her in the study and read on through the afternoon. She learned a great deal more about the Langlais family and the village in general. And there was no question that the district had a dark record of superstition and evil happenings in that bygone period. When she realized it was getting late, she left the study to go upstairs.

Count Henri and his wife, Maria, came in the front door just as she reached the hallway. They were dressed in full mourning clothes, and she at once surmised it had to do with the funeral of Therese. She was a little surprised the ceremony had been held so soon.

The Count gazed at her with sad eyes. "My wife and I have just now come from the cemetery."

"You've already had the burial?" Eve said, hinting plainly that she considered it hurried.

The Count's wife dabbed a hankie to her eyes. "We decided we should not draw the sorrow out longer. The poor child!"

The Count coughed gently. "We must not behave in a maudlin fashion. Eve is our guest, and we have no right to impose this burden of sorrow on her. The affair is over and done with. No amount of tears can do anything for Therese now."

"I would have liked to have attended the funeral," she said.

"No need," the Count said. "This has been distressing enough for you without that."

"I'd like to pay my respects at her grave," Eve insisted.

The Count nodded. "You can. It's not far from the chateau in the family cemetery. Leonard might escort you there."

"I'll speak to him about it later," she said. And starting up the stairs, she added, "I don't feel like dinner tonight. I'll have something in my room."

She went on up the stairs, leaving the two still in the entrance hall. She remained in her room until dusk arrived. Then she went downstairs to wait for Leonard. She went out onto the terrace as it was warm and she wanted to be free of the house. She had begun to feel there was an evil there that was stifling.

As she stood there she saw him walking slowly towards her through the garden. He was dressed in dark, and his handsome face wore a pained look. He came up the steps onto the terrace and took her hands in his gloved ones. Their eyes met sadly.

"I know how upset you are," he said quietly.

"I feel we are partly to blame," she blurted out.

"Nonsense," he said. "Therese was always a sullen unhappy girl. When I went back to the chapel after leaving you, I couldn't find her. I wanted to talk and reason with her. But I believe she left very soon after we saw her. She'd probably killed herself before midnight."

"I can't really believe it," Eve said in a taut voice. "Last night she stood there so much alive, and tonight she's buried."

"My uncle handled it so as to create as little scandal as possible."

She stared up at him anxiously. "Are you positive that is the reason?"

He furrowed his brow. "What other reason could there be?"

Not wanting him to accuse her of wild imaginings again, she hesitated to say what had been nagging at her mind. Instead she murmured, "I don't know."

"Let us go for a walk," he said.

"I'd like to visit her grave. Your uncle says the cemetery isn't far."

Leonard shook his head. "I won't encourage that morbidity. It would do Therese no good. Let us stroll along the cliffs instead."

She had no wish to do that. But she wanted to be with him and so she made no protest. They took the path to the cliffs, the path that the tortured Therese must surely have taken the previous night, and before darkness finally settled, they had reached the rocky eminence with its fine view of the ocean.

Once again the blond young man did what had struck her as strange when they'd walked the cliffs before. Every now and then he halted to stare out across the water. Since it was almost dark, she couldn't imagine what he was seeing.

She said, "You're doing it again?"

"What?"

"Staring out at the ocean with it nearly dark."

He smiled wanly. "I told you I have a remarkable gift of vision. I can see very clearly."

"I can't believe it."

"And yet you are ready to believe so many other incredible things," he teased her. "It is true. Just now I saw the outline of a distant ship."

Eve studied the shadowed horizon and saw nothing. "I can't see it," she announced.

"I don't expect you to," he smiled. "It's my special gift."

They did not go down to the beach but returned to the house as darkness shrouded the countryside. She told him about her reading during the day and of the dreadful fate of the first Count Leonard Langlais.

"They accused him of being a vampire," she told him. "And the girl of being a witch."

"That wasn't hard to do in those days," he said grimly.

"I believe his brother did it deliberately to get the estates. He put them both to death at the stake."

"Poor sweet Ann Crillon," the man on the bench beside her said softly.

She turned to stare at him. His gaze was fixed in the distance as if his mind was far away. She said, "Ann Crillon? Who was she?"

He at once came back to himself and gave her a melancholy look. "The girl in your story. The one who died at the stake. I'm versed in the history of the family too, you know."

"Of course," she apologized. "The girl's name wasn't given in the account I read."

"That was not the only account," he said.

"I must look for the others," she said. "I don't know

whether your uncle was offended by my leaving the party last night or not. With the tragic happenings of today he neglected to make any mention of it."

"I apologized for you," Leonard told her. "He understood."

She sighed. "I know it sounds ridiculous coming from me, a student of the black arts. But when I'm faced with an actual group involved with sorcery I find it unhealthy."

"I think the suicide of Therese has depressed you," he suggested. "That is why you feel strangely."

"No. I'm sure I felt this way before it happened."

"I have always respected your interest in the lore of evil," he said. "It shows you have a keen mind. My uncle was impressed by you from his first meeting with you in Paris."

"I'm not sure he properly understood me," she worried.

"He chose you as a possible wife for me," the blond man said gently. "And when I met you at Dinard, I knew that he had made the perfect choice."

She looked up at him. "I do like you a great deal, Leonard. But I'm doubtful if I could ever live happily here."

"Why not?"

"I've already said it. The chateau has known so much evil. I think it has become a living force here. The evil itself. The Satanists believe that is possible."

"But this is my home," he argued.

"Your uncle is the Count. He will live here until his death. And I no longer feel easy with him."

"This is not any time to debate it," he said, rising. "I must say goodnight. I've a bad headache and am not good company."

She saw that once again there was that strange burning light in his eyes. All her former fears that he might be mad returned. Mention of his headache also suggested his trouble was mental rather than physical. She asked, "Is this family illness you've suffered from mostly of a nervous nature?" It was the most polite way she could ask if the family weakness was insanity.

He at once looked stunned. "Why do you ask a question like that?"

"You needn't answer if you don't want to," she said.

"Of course I'll answer you," he said with a touch of anger. "I'm not mad now and I never have been."

Eve blushed. "I didn't mean to suggest you were. But all these strange references to hereditary illness with no explanation given upset me."

The handsome blond man relented. "I'm sorry. It's natural they should. My trouble is an illness of the blood. Didn't my uncle explain?"

"Not very well."

"Remind me to show you my medical charts," he said. "Now I really must leave you."

"You haven't kissed me goodnight."

He looked guilty. "Sorry. It's this headache. How could I forget otherwise?" And he gave her a very cursory embrace.

Then he left her abruptly. Almost as if he knew some seizure was about to take hold of him and he didn't want her to see it. She found herself badly worried. She remained there on the terrace with the distant cry of a night bird echoing in her ears in a melancholy fashion.

Again her doubts became almost panic. Only the fact she would need the Count's permission prevented her from trying to leave the fenced grounds of the chateau. She'd never get beyond that electric fence on her own. She went up to bed.

The following morning was sunny and warm. And she decided to go to the beach. She wanted to be alone to think things out, and this was difficult to do in the great mansion. Yesterday she had drowned herself in reading. But she realized she could no longer find help in escaping to the past. There were decisions she must make, and they could only be made by facing up to the events around her realistically.

She had no doubt that Count Langlais was doing everything in his power to make her marry his nephew. And while she was fond of the blond young man, there were many things concerning the family she did not fully understand. How involved Count Henri was in black magic for one. And how likely to be fatal Leonard's illness was for another. She could make no binding decision about her future until she knew the true answers to these things and others.

The Count might be angry if she left without committing herself to marry the sick young man, but he would be no less unhappy than she would be in losing the handsome Leonard. Yet she did not want to tie herself to this family without full understanding of what it would mean. She did not want to live her life at Chateau Langlais with any of its dark secrets still hidden from her.

Today she would make her decision while she sat alone on the beach. And when she saw Leonard tonight, she would let him know what she was going to do. It had to be as clear-cut as that. The tragic death of Therese had shocked her into taking this stand. She did not intend to carelessly throw away her own life.

She left the house without encountering anyone. The servants had been taught to remain discreetly in the background except when they were needed. Sometimes she would hear the echoes of their voices from the rear of the old building. But the only one she saw much of was Raol. And she still avoided him whenever possible as his eyes made her uneasy.

The beach was completely deserted. She spread out her

blanket and sat on it to stare out at the horizon. In the brilliant sunlight she could see as far as Leonard claimed he could when it was almost dark. It was a weird thing, his unusual night vision. She supposed it wasn't all that uncommon. Yet every time she saw him standing staring out at the ocean in the darkness it gave her an eerie feeling.

Absorbed in her thoughts she kept her eyes fixed straight ahead. And then she suddenly realized with a start she was no longer alone. She glanced fearfully to the right and saw it was Leonard who had silently come up to stand beside her!

Chapter Eight

"Leonard!" she gasped.

The blond handsome man in fawn sports slacks and white blouse open at the neck looked down at her with troubled eyes. "No," he said quietly.

She looked at him in bewilderment. Then she scrambled to her feet. "What is wrong?" she asked anxiously. "You must be ill and confused! You know you shouldn't be out in this sun. I'll help you back to the chateau." She made a move to take his arm.

"You don't understand," he said.

She stared at him from behind the dark glasses. And all at once it struck her. There was a subtle difference between this man and the one she'd been with last night and the other nights before. This man was healthier in appearance. His face had more tan, and there was no hint of that strange gleam in his eyes. The odd burning that sometimes gave Leonard a frightening appearance.

In a whisper, she said, "You're not Leonard."

"You saved me from telling you," was the young man's grim reply.

"Then who are you?" she demanded, at once on her guard.

He looked at her incredulously. "Don't you recognize me after all the time we spent together in Dinard?"

"In Dinard?" she echoed stupidly.

"I'm the man you spent most of those two weeks with," the blond look-alike for Leonard said earnestly.

"This is some kind of evil joke!" she protested. "Something the Count and Leonard have cooked up to taunt me about my mistaking the doctor and that old priest for other people I'd met."

"It has nothing to do with Count Langlais or his nephew, believe me," the blond man said tensely. "As a matter of fact, if we're seen together there'll be trouble. I suggest we find a place near the cliff where we can't be spied on."

Eve was still suspicious of him. Keeping him a distance from her, she demanded, "Who are you?"

"A friend. You must believe that," he said earnestly, and gazed up at the cliffs with apprehensive eyes.

"What do you want?"

"To talk to you a few minutes," he said, facing her again. "To try and explain all this. But we mustn't be seen together by any of the Chateau crowd or we'll find ourselves in danger."

She wavered in indecision. This young man who looked so familiar and yet talked like a stranger had her thoroughly confused. She would have sworn it was Leonard until she'd taken the close second look at him. Now she knew he could be the man she'd known at Dinard, but that didn't seem possible. Was he some kind of insane person, or a pawn in a macabre game the Count was playing with her?

Studying him with wary eyes, she asked, "How do I know I can trust you?"

"You'll understand that after you hear what I have to say."

"I'm listening."

"Not here," he said, staring up at the cliffs in that furtive, scared way again. "There's a kind of partially formed cave further along the shore. We can talk safely there. I'll show you."

And without giving her a chance to protest, he grasped her

by the hand and began hurrying along the sandy beach. She had an impulse to draw back, but then thought better of it. Now that the first shock of meeting him was over, she was terribly curious as to the explanation of his being Leonard's double.

They were both breathless by the time he shepherded her into a cavelike indentation in the gray cliffs. As soon as they were safely shielded from the view of anyone on the heights above, he seemed to relax.

She still kept her distance from him, gazing at him with eyes that even now held fear. She looked into the blue eyes of Leonard, the serious handsome face of Leonard, saw Leonard's wavy blond hair and his familiar lithe body and yet was supposed to believe this was someone else.

She said, "I think you are Leonard. That you and your uncle are playing another wicked trick on me."

"I can't blame you for thinking that," the young man said frankly. "My name is David Mazin. I'm an actor. Count Henri Langlais found me through a film agency in Paris. I was between engagements and he talked me into posing as his nephew for several weeks and paid me well for it."

Eve frowned as she listened. "Then it was you I met at Dinard!"

The blond man nodded. "Yes. Naturally I made the Count explain the reason for the impersonation before I would agree to it. He told me about his nephew who suffered from a rare disease that had plagued their family for years. He explained that the young man had recently suffered a bad attack and they'd almost given up hope of his recovery."

"The real Leonard."

"Yes. The real Leonard. The Count went on to tell me he'd met a girl he felt would make an ideal wife for his ailing nephew. But he was afraid she'd never become interested in an invalid. So he'd searched out a double to win her attention. I was the double, and he needed me to play the role of his nephew and make you fall in love."

Eve's throat tightened. "You managed that well."

"I'm sorry, Eve," the actor said penitently. "The fact I'm here should prove that. It's not without risk, I assure you. The Count first brought me here for a week to study his nephew. I found Leonard a rather pleasant if melancholy man. It made my impersonation a less unpleasant task. If I could be the means of a young woman becoming interested in him and maybe marrying him, it would bring some happiness to a life doomed to chronic illness. By the time the Count took me to Dinard I knew my man well enough to play the part perfectly."

"Without any regard for my welfare," she said bitterly.

"I didn't know you then, Eve," he said, his eyes meeting hers and the regret in them undeniable. "I began to worry as the two weeks came to an end. I decided to tell you the truth when we made our excursion to St. Malo. But I think the Count guessed what I had in mind. He's very sharp. When I returned to the hotel the night before our planned visit to the island, he ordered me to pack and leave with him."

"You still should have left me some warning."

"I know," he sighed. "I was confused and in a difficult situation. He paid my fee and drove me back to Paris. I left the following weekend to make a film in Italy. All the while I was there, I worried about you."

Stunned by his revelations, Eve said, "You knew I would be invited here. That I would meet Leonard and think it was you."

"I tried to ease my conscience by telling myself you'd soon detect the difference between us. That the deception wouldn't fool you. But then I realized you'd not seen us together and there had been a time lapse to further blur your memory. I began to feel worse and worse about it. Knowing you were being victimized and I was responsible."

"I'm surprised you admit it," she said, torn between the love she'd known for him and the letdown of hearing his confession.

He smoothed back his blond hair in an actor's gesture of distress. "I don't expect you to forgive me easily. But I swear that as soon as I finished with the film I came directly back to the village. I lived at the inn for a little while until I found a way to get into the estate. I hired a fisherman to bring me here to the beach last night. Most of them won't venture near the place since they think there's a curse on it. But I knew I'd never get by the gates or that electric fence. I talked this old fellow into bringing me and hid until I saw you. When I was at the chateau, I found an outside cellar entrance leading to Leonard's section of the castle. I'm going up there later and try and find what is going on in there. I think it is something evil. The Count has ties with a group of Satanists. I'm afraid this business of arranging a marriage between you and his nephew is not as innocent as he pretended. I mean to find out. But first I had to warn you."

"It's an incredible story."

"But the truth," he said sincerely.

"Then I ought to try and escape at once."

"Not yet," he said. "It would mean a showdown with the Count before you got outside those electrically charged barriers. And you might wind up in worse trouble."

"How could I be in worse trouble?"

"We don't know yet," he warned her. "For the present you're in no physical danger. All the Count wants is your promise to marry his nephew."

Her face shadowed with fear. "I don't understand his illness. I think Leonard may be mad. At least he may have mad spells."

"It's possible," the actor said.

"I'm so frightened," she said. "I don't know whether I can go on pretending any longer. I'm bound to give away that I know the truth about him and the deception played on me."

"Not if you're careful."

"More than that. Leonard may be a murderer. Therese supposedly killed herself by throwing herself over the cliffs. I think he may have done it."

David Mazin looked shocked. "Therese is dead! I counted on some help from her."

"Perhaps that is why she is dead," Eve hinted.

"There was no word of it in the village."

"The Count kept it very quiet. She was buried on the estate yesterday."

The blond actor scowled. "That's suspicious in itself. And you really think Leonard may have killed her?"

"I'm only guessing," she said. "He and Therese had a bitter quarrel early that evening. He spoke of putting her in her place. He could have done it."

"That does make the situation more urgent," David Mazin said grimly. "I'll have to step up my program and try and get into Leonard's apartment this afternoon or sometime in the night."

"What do you expect to find out?"

"At this moment I can't guess," he said unhappily. "Leonard seemed normal enough most of the time I spent with him. But madness often comes in occasional spells. And he was very melancholy. It could be the Count is trying to have you marry a lunatic."

"I'm terrified," she said.

"From now on you know I'm here on the estate," he said.

"And I'll somehow keep in touch with you."

"But suppose they discover you're here?" she worried. "They could kill you and no one would ever know. The police, the doctor, even that old priest are linked with the Count in his group of Devil-worshippers!"

"I'll be extra careful," he promised her. "I've got a hiding place and food and drink to see me through. I should have the mystery solved by tomorrow morning. Will you meet me here around ten?"

"Yes."

"If I'm not here, leave at once and come back an hour or so later," he instructed her. "Something might detain me. And be sure they don't find out you know the truth."

"I'm not trained as an actress," she reminded him. "And I'm sick with fear as well."

"You're too deep in this now to do anything but see it through."

Her eyes met his, and she said bitterly, "So I am. This is what you accomplished so well at Dinard!"

David moved close to her and took her in his arms. "Eve, you must know I'm here only because I'm in love with you. I can't let you marry Leonard or anyone else. I want you for myself."

His passionate declaration swept away any remaining resentment she had. And the ardent kiss from his warm lips was a thrilling reminder of the wonderful days they'd spent together at the seaside resort. In the security of his arms she was able to admit that she loved this man. This man who had come to rescue her from the nightmare world into which she'd stumbled.

Releasing her, he said, "Now we must go."

She nodded. "Ten tomorrow. Here."

"That's it," he agreed. Again he took her by the hand and

led her out of their hiding spot. He'd only taken a few steps out on the beach when he dodged quickly back and made a warning gesture to her to keep silent. She obeyed him and stared out at the beach with haunted eyes as they huddled in the shadow of the odd rock formation.

They'd only been watching a moment or two when the hulking form of the brutish Raol came shuffling by. Every so often he halted and stared around him as if he were looking for somebody. They waited until he'd gone by and had time to get a distance away.

David touched his lips to hers again and smiled encouragingly. "Good girl!" he said. "I was afraid you might scream."

"I wanted to," she admitted.

"Now!" he said sharply. "You go back to your blanket and sun for a little. I'm going to take a path up the cliff." They both left their hiding place with him going one way and her another.

When she reached the spot where her blanket and things were, she stood and looked around to see if there was any sign of the actor or even of Raol. But the beach seemed empty again. Sinking down on her blanket, she stared out at the blue sunlit ocean and tried to straighten it all out in her mind.

Learning the truth about the impersonation had cleared many things up for her. But she agreed with David that there were nuances to the situation of which neither of them were fully aware yet. There was more to this than a fond uncle trying to find a suitable mate for an invalid nephew. And perhaps the key to it all rested in the cult of Satanism flourishing in the village of Langlais.

She was to think more about this that afternoon when she went to the study to do some reading and found the elderly but still handsome Count Henri there at his desk. The white-haired man with the aquiline face rose with a smile.

"Come in and join me," he invited her.

She hesitated. She was afraid to be too long in his company now in case he might sense a change in her. "No need to disturb you," she said. "I was only going to pick out another book to read."

"I insist that you do that," he said, with a gesture towards the shelves of books that lined the walls of the room from floor to ceiling. "We have enough of them."

"Thank you," she said, going over to one of the shelves and scanning some of the book titles.

"The family histories are to your left," Count Henri said. "If I remember rightly, you were reading about the original Leonard Langlais who became Count for a period."

"Yes," she turned to the white-haired man. "He was Count until his younger brother accused him of serving the Devil. Being a vampire, if I'm not mistaken. At any rate he had him executed and took over the estate himself."

The thin, sensitive face of the elderly man held a bitter smile. "It was Count Clarence who did that. He was something of a villain, you know. Later accounts vindicate Leonard completely and say it was Clarence who was the evildoer. That he executed Ann Crillon, the witch, because he had been her lover. And he accused Leonard of the crime for which he himself was guilty."

Eve lost some of her nervousness in her interest in what the Count was telling her. "Then Count Leonard never was a vampire?"

Count Henri sighed and looked speculative. "I have read two different views concerning him. One claims he was indeed a vampire because Clarence had the witch, Ann Crillon, place the curse on him. But that he was an innocent victim of witchcraft rather than evil. The other story is that he escaped the vampire curse because of the purity of his heart, and it was Clarence who did the evil things for which he was blamed. I've never made up my mind which version is the true one. You can take your choice."

"You and your group must have made a thorough study of the case," she suggested.

The Count smiled benignly. "There are so many cases to authenticate. We have barely touched the surface of them. I'm sorry you had to leave the party. My friends enjoyed meeting you, and many of them wanted to discuss medieval black art with you."

"I was stricken by a bad headache."

"So I understand," he said casually, as if it was something he didn't believe. "You missed a fine musicale and a most interesting performance of a true Black Mass ritual."

"A performance?" she questioned.

"Well, of course it wouldn't be the real thing," he said with an easy laugh. "Our obsession with Lucifer doesn't go quite that far. But based on the old accounts we have managed to produce a dramatic version of a mass of this nature."

A strong feeling that it had been the real thing offered as a theatrical performance filled her. In a quiet voice, she said, "I'm sorry I missed it."

His hypnotic eyes were fixed on hers. "Of course the success of the night was fatally marred by the suicide of Therese. Poor girl."

His eyes boring into her increasing her nervousness. Turning away to pretend she was studying the shelf of books, she asked, "Could the atmosphere of the Black Mass have depressed her?"

"I think not," the Count replied. "Therese always had a neurotic streak. I assume it finally became true madness."

She hastily pulled a book from the shelf to draw his attention away from her uneasiness. She read the title aloud,

"Antidote against Atheism."

"By Henry More," the man at her elbow said in a dry voice. "It was published in the seventeenth century. I have read it enough to memorize it."

"I have never seen it before," she said, turning its pages.

"It's a true classic," the Count told her. "About a vampire in Silesia. His name was Johannes Cuntius. He was killed in an accident when he was about sixty. At the time of his death, a black cat rushed into the room where his body was resting, jumped up on the corpse and violently scratched the face."

She glanced at the solemn face of the Count. "An example of the cat as Devil."

"Yes. There was a thunderstorm as the man was being buried. But it ended as soon as he was placed in the ground. However, soon after the burial there were rumors that his ghost stalked the village by night. There were tales of milk being changed into blood, of young women strangled with strange fang marks on their necks, of children being taken from their cradles and altar cloths being soiled by blood."

She shivered in spite of herself. "All the usual vampire lore."

"Of course you are familiar with these things," he said. "They decided to dig up the body, and when they did, his skin was found to be tender and florid. His joints were by no means stiff. And later, when a staff was placed between his fingers, they closed around it and held it firmly. He could open and shut his eyes, and when a vein was punctured in his leg, blood shot out from it. This was after the body had been in the grave six months."

"What was done with the corpse?"

"The body was cut up and dismembered by order of the authorities," the Count said. "The story goes that it offered strong resistance. But when the task was completed and the remains consigned to flames, the specter ceased to molest the natives."

Eve closed the book and stared at it. "It is a typical story."

"Yes. There are many of them. Voodooism and Obi are cults in which the living dead play a major role. Corpses are often used in their rites."

She retumed the book to its place on the shelf. "I'm not in the mood for this today," she said.

"I understand," the elderly man agreed. "It is unfortunate that my nephew's illness prevents him from joining you in the daytime. You had such a fine time together on the beach at Dinard."

She had to almost bite her tongue to hold back from saying that he had seemed an entirely different person then. Instead she told him, "Yes. His absence does make my days lonely."

Count Henri smiled in understanding. "Father Boulanger was curious as to when you two would announce your plans to marry. He felt strongly you would make a fine pair."

She looked down. "That is something Leonard and I will have to discuss further."

"Don't put it off too long," the elderly man urged.

She excused herself and hurriedly left him. Now that she knew about the deception, she felt wary of everyone in the old castle, conscious that they were manipulating her for their own benefit. She went up to her bedroom and thought about David Mazin. She wondered if he would have luck getting into the castle and whether he'd discover anything worthwhile.

While she was sitting there, a cautious knock came on the door. She went over to see who it was, and Maria was standing there. The Count's wife entered with an apologetic expression on her pale face. "I hope you won't mind my intruding."

"Not at all," Eve said.

"What sad days these are for all of us," Maria said.

"Yes." She had the feeling the woman was there for a purpose but was hesitant about getting on with it.

Maria advanced further into the room and glanced around. "Are you happy here?"

"It's very nice," she said.

The older woman gave her a nervous look. "I was thinking that Therese's room is vacant now. You could move in there if you liked. I believe it has a somewhat nicer view."

Eve felt a surge of panic. What new evil were they planning? She quickly said, "I'd prefer to remain here."

Maria looked slightly disappointed. "Just as you say, my dear. You do have all your things arranged in here."

"It's perfectly all right."

She nodded. "Whatever you think. I have just been going through Therese's possessions. We are surely going to miss her. She was like our own daughter. Her father was the Count's best friend. There was no one else to take the girl when he died. So we brought her here and raised her as one of the family."

"She was beautiful," Eve said.

Maria looked distressed. "And such a way for that beauty to end." She moved towards the door and then turned as if in an afterthought, "There is something else I wanted to speak to you about."

"Yes?"

The pale woman smiled sadly. "I want to give you something that belonged to Therese. It is a shame that it should remain in a jewel box without being used. It was a present from the Count." And she reached in a pocket of her dark blue dress and held out a gold necklace in the palm of her hand. "It's very old and exquisitely designed. Please accept it."

"I'd rather not," she protested.

Maria smiled faintly. "You mustn't refuse me. I've discussed this with the Count, and he was insistent that you should have it." She pressed the necklace closer to her.

Reluctantly Eve took the string of what seemed golden beads. As she held the necklace in her own hands, she saw that the tiny sections were not beads but perfectly formed golden beetles!

She gasped. "It's much too valuable!"

"The Count and I want you to have it."

Eve stared at the beautifully designed piece, and her mind was whirling. She knew only too well the role that beetles played in Black Magic charms. Whether the necklace had belonged to Therese or not, it was liable to have a purpose. The gift could be meant to protect her or place a curse on her. And she would be inclined to believe it was the latter.

"I'd rather not take it," she continued to try to hand the necklace back to the older woman.

But Maria was already at the door. "You must," she smiled. "And wear it! It will please the Count." The woman closed the door after her.

Eve stood there alone with the necklace. She had no intention of wearing it. And she could only hope that whatever spell it was meant to exert would be rendered useless as long as she didn't put it on.

She went over to the dresser drawer, and opening it, found her jewel box and put the necklace in with her other jewelry. Meanwhile, she'd keep making up excuses for not wearing it.

The big test came for her at dusk that evening. She was in the living room of the old mansion, standing looking at the pen sketch of Count Leonard of long ago when the modern Leonard came up beside her.

Dressed in white flannels, he looked less haggard than the

night before. He smiled at her and said, "You seem interested in that drawing."

She turned and said, "It is so much like you."

"My uncle says the same thing," Leonard said, studying it. "I think the resemblance is scant."

She asked him, "What happened to your father and mother? I've never heard you or any of the others mention them."

The blond man looked taken aback. "I must have spoken to you about them."

"Not that I can remember." She was watching him closely.

He frowned. "They died in an epidemic of a disease that struck here when I was only a baby. I don't remember them at all. Uncle Henri and Aunt Maria brought me up."

"What sort of epidemic?" She went on with her questioning because she was convinced his story wasn't true, that this had something to do with the mystery shrouding the chateau.

"A virulent influenza," he said without conviction. "Many people were stricken with it at the time."

She turned her gaze to the drawing. "You and he had something in common, it seems."

"Why do you say that?" his tone was startled.

Eve gave him a measuring look. "When I was reading the history of your family, I discovered that the parents of the first Count Leonard both died of plague while he was of an early age. He and his younger brother were left in charge of a cousin."

Leonard's handsome face had taken on a bleak look. "I'm afraid I've forgotten the story."

She decided to try a stab in the dark. "But you talked to me a lot about your family during our holiday together at Dinard."

The blond man shrugged. "I had plenty of leisure for it then."

And Eve knew a moment of inward triumph. She had proven David Mazin's story to be right by trapping Leonard into making this statement. Of course his family history had never been mentioned at Dinard!

Chapter Nine

There was humidity and an eerie silence in the air the next morning. The clouds were heavy and an ominous shade of gray. Eve hesitated about going to the beach, but she knew she must keep her rendezvous with the handsome young film actor. There was no point in changing to her bathing suit with the day so threatening. She decided to merely walk down to the beach in her regular things.

She was careful to leave the house when there was no one around to notice her. And then she hurried through the gardens and went briskly along the path to the cliffs and the beach. Once she was out of sight of the chateau, she felt easier. And she began to think of her meeting with David and what he might have to tell her.

Being with Leonard last night had proven an ordeal. Once she'd trapped him in a lie confirming her suspicions that he was not the same man she'd fallen in love with at Dinard, the time with him became a trial. He had also been oddly restless again, and when he said goodnight to her, she'd noticed that strange gleam in his eyes.

He'd talked to her of marriage, and she'd refused to discuss it. He'd pointed out that his uncle and aunt were elderly, and the chateau and all the property belonging to the estate would be his.

"I'm not well enough to manage it alone," he'd told her. "I need a wife like you to take on some of the responsibility."

"And I would never be happy here," she'd protested.

He had shown amazement. "But you are interested in the

past. You have made history and witchcraft your subjects at the university. A place like this should have great interest for you."

"I find it hard to explain," she'd said. "But I don't want you to take it for granted that we'll be married." She had wanted to tell him the truth, that she'd discovered the deception that had been played on her. But that could wait.

The dark, threatening morning seemed in keeping with her errand. She had begun to wonder if David Mazin's advice had been sound. Had she been wise to remain at the chateau? It was a question. The truth was she'd not had much choice, regardless of the danger she knew herself to be in. The estate was a guarded fortress and no one got in or out without the Count's permission. The only one who'd managed it was the young actor. And now he might have stumbled into a trap.

There was a rumble of thunder as she reached the beach. The ocean was choppy with angry flecks of white caps. Moving quickly, she kept close to the rocky face of the cliff until she reached the cave rendezvous where she'd met the actor the day before. He was not there!

Additional rumblings of thunder came, but the storm could be a long way off. She hoped it might pass the area and debated why the blond man was so late.

Then she saw him coming quickly along the beach. He was wearing the disguise he'd mentioned. The dark glasses and black wig changed his appearance a great deal.

"Sorry I'm late," he said in his familiar voice. It was enough to reassure her.

"It's all right," she said. "You look so different in disguise."

"I put on the wig in case anyone saw me. Cut down the risk of them knowing who it was. When we talked yesterday, I forgot to tell you about the trouble in the village."

"What trouble?"

"Happened before I left. A girl was killed by a tourist's car in the small hours of the morning. The driver was a German, and according to him, the girl came staggering across the street in front of his car. He didn't have time to stop. He claimed she was in a kind of daze. At any rate, the car struck and killed the girl."

"Why should she be wandering in the street at that hour?"

David looked grim. "That's why the villagers are so upset. They believe she'd been attacked first. There were weird teeth marks on her throat. A number of other young village women have been attacked and found in a dazed state with the same marks."

She stared at him incredulously. "You mean they're starting the vampire talk again?"

"That's it," he said. "The majority of the villagers believe in black magic. And they could be right."

"Why do you say that?" She had noticed the hint of bleak conviction in his tone.

"I can show you better than I can explain," David said with a meaningful glance. "There is something at the chateau I want you to see."

"Then you did get in to look around."

"Yes. I filed off the lock on that side door of the wing nearest the ocean. The one where Leonard Langlais has his apartment. After that it was easy. When I left, I fixed the lock in place so no one would notice that it had been tampered with."

"What now?"

"I'm going directly there, and I want you to walk back by the other path and join me when you reach the chateau. I'll be waiting by that side door for you."

"Dare you go back again?"

"I think so. I have no choice," he said soberly. "It's something I have to do."

The thunder rumbled loudly. This time it was closer. "I think we're about to have a storm," she said fearfully.

"All the better," he said. "There is less chance of anyone being out to notice us."

"I think I'm losing my nerve," she confessed.

"Not much wonder," he said. "But we're near the end of it, I think."

"Last night was torment. The Count and his wife can be so sly. And I couldn't help resenting Leonard, knowing that he is an impostor."

"In a sense," the actor said, "from another point of view, I was the impostor."

"You're the one who interests me," she said. "I have always had a strange feeling about him."

"Understandable," he said. And glancing out at the dark sky, he told her, "I think we'd better get on our way. The storm could break any moment."

They left the hiding place to take separate ways again. As Eve hurried along the path, the thunder came heavily and there was a sharp flash of lightning. At the same instant a huge drop of rain pelted her cheek. She increased her pace.

Reaching the gardens, she stared up at the stately gray turrets of the Chateau Langlais outlined against the dark sky. The thunder and lightning came once more, with the flash of blue casting an eerie glare on the ancient castle. How many such storms had it known in its long history, she wondered. It began to rain heavily in a sudden cloudburst, and she ran towards a side path leading to the wing of the old building the actor had mentioned.

Stumbling along on the wet ground, she at last found him

standing by a cellar door. He quickly led her down several stone steps, and they entered the black underground room.

Closing the door, he whispered, "It isn't far to the steps and the apartment Leonard uses."

She kept close to him as he led her across the dark cellar to a flight of stone stairs. "Is there anyone here with him?" she whispered.

"Not that I noticed before," he said. "He spends his days alone."

"He said he did. Any noise distracts him."

He made no reply as they had emerged in a shadowed corridor. Tiny windows in its stone walls revealed the blue flash of the lightning as the storm grew in fury. The actor continued to hold onto her arm as they hurried down the corridor. When they reached the end of it, he opened an oak door, and she found herself in a large room with tapestries and rich furniture. It seemed clear the young invalid lived in luxurious surroundings.

David made a sign for her to be silent and led her through the great living room to a smaller chamber beyond. This was almost in darkness. It was not until the lightning came once more that she had any hint of the way it was furnished, and then she found this most unusual.

The lengthy blue glare revealed only what looked to be a great high chest on the floor in the far corner of the room and a single plain chair by it. The lightning faded as the thunder came with a frightening loudness. She gave the actor a nervous glance and saw an odd expression on his handsome face. He had removed his dark glasses but he still wore the black wig.

The sound of the rain from outside followed the thunder and she spoke over it to ask, "What sort of room is this?"

"This is where he rests during the day," he told her.

"I don't understand!"

"You will!" was his grim assurance.

And as he said this, he moved forward to the big ornamented chest. And giving her a look of warning over his shoulder, he proceeded to laboriously lift the heavy lid of the chest until it swung all the way back. He turned to her again.

"Come here," he said quietly.

She studied him with terrified eyes as she did what he asked. Moving slowly, she approached the great chest bathed in shadows. It was a coincidence that as she bent to look down into it the lightning came again, and she clearly saw Leonard resting in it, head on a pillow, hands folded on his chest, exactly like a corpse! She gave a loud gasp of fear and staggered back. The actor was there to support her and turn her away from the chest.

"You've seen enough," he said.

Her hands had automatically come up to her eyes to hide the ugly sight of the corpselike rigid face in the depths of the chest. Now she lowered them and glanced back at the corner of the room. "It's a coffin," she said in an awed tone. "He's sleeping there in a coffin!"

"A kind of sleep," the actor said significantly.

She looked at him wide-eyed. "Meaning?"

"There is your vampire who has been terrorizing the village all this time. You're a student of the black arts. You must be familiar with such cases."

Eve nodded slowly. "I should have guessed. It's no disease that keeps him from the sunlight. It's the curse of the vampire. He's only alive from dusk to dawn."

"And that's what the Count hoped you would marry," David Mazin said bitterly. "And to think I helped him with it."

She stood there in the near darkness of the tomblike room.

Touching his arm, she said, "You've helped me now."

"And we've found out the truth about what is going on here. How would this Leonard be turned into the thing he is?"

Eve shook her head. "It could be a curse. The bite of a bat that wasn't a bat but one of the living dead in that guise. There are many ways. I couldn't begin to guess."

"The Count may have been responsible. He's the leader of the Satanists."

"I don't think he would do this to his nephew," she said. And then a strange expression crossed her face. "You know an ancestor of Leonard's also bore the vampire curse. It could be something that has come down through the line." She paused as another horrifying thought came to her. She gave the young actor an awed look and in a lower voice added, "Or this could be that same ancestor. A vampire can live on forever unless it is destroyed!"

The lightning and thunder came again before David could make any reply to this, but she saw the look of concern on his handsome face. He gazed at the chest in which the body was resting.

As the thunder ended, he said, "The Count has to be helping him. I have no doubt he comes here every night and releases him from the chest. And probably sees that he is safely back in it at dawn."

She nodded. Shocked by their macabre discovery, "It must have been Leonard who attacked that girl last night and sent her wandering in a daze to be struck by a car."

"Without a question," he agreed. "I'll close the chest and we'll get away from here."

Eve watched as he lowered the heavy lid. The ghastly vision of the rigid form of the Count's nephew in his corpse-like state flashed across her mind. And she remembered the cold lips of the haggard blond man. And the hands he kept covered with white gloves. These should have been warnings to her if she'd ever had the slightest idea of the true nature of Leonard.

She had studied many accounts of vampires, and Leonard fitted exactly into the pattern. The Count had been wily enough to spread the story that his nephew was afflicted with the disease in which people became allergic to the sun. Because there was such a disease, she had not bothered to question his story. Surely she had not imagined that this nephew was one of the living dead!

David returned to her, and they went out into the big room again. He said, "Now you see why he hired me. His nephew didn't dare to leave the chateau or attempt to court you by daylight."

The thunder and lightning had eased, and the storm now seemed to have settled into a heavy rain. She stood there, nauseated by her discovery. The silent apartment seemed to have the dusty smell of death about it.

"This is a horrible place," she murmured. "I must get away."

David gave her a significant look. "Our work isn't finished yet."

She stared at him. "What do you mean?"

"We must confront the Count with our discovery. We'll go to him together."

"He'll deny everything!"

"Let him try," the actor said sternly. "We'll call the police and not even his exalted position will explain away that thing in the chest."

"I don't know," she said, her tone faltering.

"We can't just run off and leave that monster to go on killing," the actor argued. "If we do that, we'll be guilty as well."

"I hadn't thought about it that way."

The young actor gave her a questioning look. "How do you destroy a vampire?"

Her eyes met his solemnly. "A stake of hawthorn through the heart is best."

"There must be some hawthorn on the estate," David said grimly.

She began to see what he had in mind. "You're going to tell the Count what we know and threaten to expose him if he doesn't destroy his nephew?"

"The vampire!" David corrected her.

"He won't do it."

"He'll have no choice. I'll take care of it myself."

Eve gazed at him with frightened eyes. "You don't know his powers! How diabolical he can be. He'll somehow stop your carrying out your plan."

"The first thing to do is face him with what we've found," the actor maintained. "After that we can decide how to handle him judging by his reaction."

"Don't underestimate him," Eve warned the actor.

They left the wing where the vampire slept and went on to the main section of the big mansion. She had never truly realized the size of the chateau before. It had an endless number of rooms in the various wings. She could conceive being lost there if you hadn't some previous knowledge of the layout.

David, still wearing the black wig, walked sedately at her side. They reached the entrance hall of the main building, and she glanced in the living room and saw no one there. The place was shadowed because of the storm outside. Rain drummed down against the windows and the awnings.

She gave David a knowing look. "He's probably in the study. That is where he spends most of the mornings."

"Go ahead," the actor told her.

Now she showed the way, and when she came to the open study door, saw that the elderly Count was seated in an easy chair by the fireplace in the study. A candle on the table beside him had been lit to provide light for his reading. His aquiline face wore an intent expression as he seemed absorbed in the leather-bound book in his lap. The flickering glow of the candle was no defense against the shadows of the rest of the study. It could have been night.

Eve stepped inside the room with a sober expression on her pretty face. She said nothing for a moment, but stood there gazing at him with sad eyes. Meanwhile David remained unseen in the corridor.

Suddenly aware of her presence, the white-haired man looked up. His questioning expression was replaced by a smile as he recognized her in the shadows.

"So it is you, Eve," he said. "I was worried about you. Raol told me you had gone to the beach. I thought you might be caught in the storm."

"I just managed to get back before the worst of it broke," she said in a dull voice.

"I can see that the experience was trying," the Count said, standing up. He made an impressive figure in the limited glow of light provided by the single candle. "I have been delving into the works of Francesco Guazzo. An interesting fellow. He claimed that witches could control not only rain and hail and wind, but even lightning, with God's permission."

Eve looked at him directly. "I know the truth, Count Langlais."

He frowned. "The truth?"

"About your nephew."

The white-haired man placed his book on the table beside the candle and regarded her with concern. "What are you trying to say to me?"

This was the cue for actor David Mazin to present himself. He had taken off his wig and looked incredibly like the unfortunate Leonard. He moved a step past her to confront the dignified aristocrat.

"We meet again, Count Langlais," he said.

The Count looked stunned. But he quickly gained some control of his upset feelings, and turning to Eve, demanded, "Who is this impertinent fellow? He looks uncommonly like my nephew, but I know it isn't he."

Dave laughed harshly. "That's a neat bit of acting. But it's too late. Eve knows I'm the one you introduced her to at Dinard. And she knows why."

"What mad story are you concocting?" the Count said drawing himself up angrily.

Eve spoke up, "We've just come from Leonard's apartment. David opened the chest and I saw him. I'm not as versed in black magic as you, but I know enough to recognize a vampire."

Her words brought about a startling change in the proud old aristocrat. The weary, handsome face seemed to suddenly crumple in despair, and clasping his hands before him, the Count sank down in the easy chair and rested his head on his raised hands.

David Mazin said sternly, "We know that your nephew has been stalking the countryside attacking young women. That he probably killed Therese because she was ready to expose him. And only last night a girl lost her life as a result of one of his cruel attacks."

The old man sat there with his head bent for several long moments without making any reply. Then he slowly lifted his head, and offering them a pleading look, said, "I beg that you don't jump to any quick conclusions. First, hear my story."

"We will not wait until another dusk," the actor warned him. "The vampire must be put to rest."

"Please!" the Count begged. And he directed his next words to her. "I am the last of my line, Eve. When I die there are no other members of the Langlais family to take the title and carry on here at the chateau. It means an end of a great family after hundreds of years."

She said, "What has that got to do with it?"

"It may make you understand about Leonard, and what you saw in his apartment," the Count said. "You know I have done a vast amount of research in the history of our family and also the black arts. One day in going through some ancient diaries, I found a reference to a chest hidden in the room below the torture chamber. You will remember I stumbled through the trapdoor leading to it that day you were with me?"

"Yes," she said, having no idea what he might be leading up to.

"I hope this is pertinent," David intervened. "We don't want to waste time."

"It is most pertinent," the old aristocrat assured him. "Following the hint in the diary, I investigated the hidden room and found the chest." He paused. "I also found the preserved body of a man in it. The body of the first Leonard Langlais, Count of our line. More than a century ago his brother had given him a poisonous potion and buried him in the chest in that secret room. But through the intervention of a witch, the potion was changed. Instead of poison Leonard was given a draught that would keep him at rest until someone roused him." The old man glanced at her. "Do you know the incantation of Assurbanipal?"

"No," she said.

"I knew it was what would work best in bringing my

ancestor out of his long sleep," the Count told them. "I sprinkled the enchanted herbs over his body and repeated the incantation: 'Hearken to my prayer. Free me from my bewitchment. Loosen my sin. Let there be turned aside whatever evil may come to cut off my life.' I waited there in the darkness after I had said the words. I thought I had failed. And then there was a slight rustling sound from the coffin. A second later a thin, veined hand clutched the side of it, and very slowly Leonard Langlais raised himself up. He opened his eyes and told me who he was, and I told him I was present Count of the line."

"Do you expect us to listen to this story?" David Mazin demanded angrily. "It is merely a pack of lies to excuse what your mad nephew has done!"

Eve gave the actor a warning glance. "I think we should hear what he has to say."

The Count gave her a grateful look. "Thank you," he said. "It was about dusk when Leonard left his coffin. I showed him around the house and grounds. And he told me that he had been given the vampire curse and might live on forever as one of the walking dead. His only regret was that he had not been able to father a son. And it was then I had my inspiration. Why not pass off this long dead man as my nephew and try to find him a suitable wife? His child could carry on the line. He promised that once the child was born, he would submit to being destroyed. He had no wish to live on indefinitely as one of the cursed."

"And it was then that you met me and decided I might make him a wife?" Eve suggested.

"Not immediately after," the Count said sadly. "It took some time to allow Leonard to become adjusted to this modern day. He had to learn the manners, modes and speech of our time. I spent many hours helping him, as did Maria and Therese. It was then that Therese became infatuated with him and asked to bear his child. But he refused her. He insisted he would marry only someone he could really love."

"Why did you pick me?" Eve wanted to know.

"That night when I first met you in the dungeon cafe I secretly snapped a picture of you on infrared film. When I showed it to him and told him you were versed in witchcraft, he was enthusiastic and at once decided you could be the proper one to marry him."

David gave the old man a disdainful look. "And I suppose you're going to tell us that is when you decided to hire me."

"What you've said is correct. I went to Paris and searched the files of actors' agencies until I found a young man who was a double for the unfortunate Leonard. I took this young man partially into my confidence and had him meet Leonard and make a study of him." The Count eyed David. "And I must say you played the role well."

"I had no idea then what it could cost Eve," David told him.

The Count spread his hands. "I do not see that I was conspiring to do her great harm. In spite of his vampire curse, Leonard is a man of charm. He would make a tender husband, and when she presented him with a son, he would vanish from the scene. I would make it look as if he'd died in an accident. Eve would be a young and wealthy widow bearing an honored name. She would have little difficulty finding a husband and the Langlais line would be secure in her son."

Eve had been somewhat touched by the old man's story. And she could understand why he had acted in this way in his desperation to keep the family alive. But she also knew that his scheme had been evil and directed against her.

She said, "Yet you knew that Leonard could live only by nightly feasting on human blood. That he had killed for such blood in the past and would kill again if he needed to."

The Count looked sad. "I tried to close my eyes to that aspect of it. I warned him against violence. And I backed him up with my knowledge of black magic, as did the circle of my friends."

"Friends like Dr. Jardin and Father Boulanger," she said with meaning. "I'm sure they helped you cast a spell over me and make me agree to come here. The pills of Dr. Devereaux and the spider in that cameo had an evil purpose."

The Count's face hardened. "I will not incriminate my friends."

"But we know that the chateau has become the headquarters of a Satanist circle," the young actor said bitterly. "And you have used these people to help the vampire."

"I did what I thought was right," Count Henri Langlais said with quiet dignity. He stood up to face them. "I am not a criminal. I do not have to tell you that. I have explained my position in this as fully as I can."

David said, "You know the authorities must be called in. This evil ring of yours must be broken up."

"My friends are merely hobbyists," the old man protested. "They do no harm."

"The police will be interested in hearing about them just the same," David said.

The Count looked distressed again. "Can't we settle this without further disgrace of the name of Langlais?"

Eve gave him a solemn look. "There is only one chance. If you agree to our terms."

The Count frowned. "What are they?"

"Leonard must die at once. You must drive a stake of hawthorn through his heart before he can wake tonight."

Chapter Ten

The Count's thin aristocratic face was a study in despair in the flickering light of the candle. He spread his hands in a gesture of appeal. "You are asking me to destroy all I have worked for?"

"It's that or the police," David told him.

The Count turned to her. "You are making me end the line of Langlais."

She said, "Have you thought of the hazard of allowing a vampire to sire a child. Suppose the baby should be born with the stigma of his father. The lore of witchcraft tells of this happening."

"The odds are against it," the Count retorted. "I'm sure a child produced by Leonard and you would have been healthy and normal."

"I wouldn't care to take the chance," she told him.

David showed impatience. "We're wasting time."

The old aristocrat eyed them in silence for a moment. Then in a resigned voice, he said, "Very well, I agree."

Eve felt a deep relief. She had liked the Count in many ways and was happy to find him reasonable. She could feel no regrets in destroying the unhappy creature in the coffin; he was a menace. And the pleasant facets of his personality had so merged in her mind with David that she would feel in an odd way that the unhappy Leonard lived on.

"As Eve says, it must be done before dusk," David cautioned the old man.

"At dusk," the Count corrected him.

David frowned. "Why?"

"That is the precise moment to destroy a vampire," the Count explained. "Immediately before the time of waking. It is a well known fact." He turned to her. "You must have heard about it?"

"It is true," she said with some hesitation. "Though I think that any time would do."

"I say the sooner the better," was David's opinion.

"If I'm to agree, it must be done my way," the white-haired man said with a touch of his usual authority.

Eve gave David a helpless look. "It can't make all that much difference."

"Very well," David said. "At dusk. What about the hawthorn?"

"I'll send out Raol to find a suitable tree," the Count said. "You can sharpen the point and drive it through his heart. I'll merely stand by as a witness."

Eve swallowed hard. "I suppose I should be there."

"It is a barbarous business and not fit for a woman's eyes," the Count warned her. "You'll be haunted by it forever if you insist on being a spectator."

David gave her a troubled look. "I think the Count is right," he said. "You let us take care of this."

"Very well," she said. "But the stake must pierce his heart."

"I'll make sure of that," the young actor said grimly.

"The burial should take place tonight," the Count said. "If the rain ends I'll have Raol look after the grave. We can put Leonard in his final resting place in the dark hours."

David shrugged. "I don't care what happens once we've destroyed him."

The Count said, "Then it is settled."

"I'll want to leave," Eve told him.

The white-haired man smiled sadly, "I see no need for you to rush away. Maria and I are going to be very lonely here."

"I have to return to Paris," David said. "I have a film to do. She can leave with me."

"Whatever you like," the old man said in a resigned tone. "But now I must go and instruct Raol about finding the hawthorn and cutting it down." With a slight bow he left the study.

She and David went out to the living room where they sat in a quiet corner discussing all that had happened and their future. David was optimistic about his film career and planned to go to Paris the following day to discuss a part. In spite of the gruesome work that was ahead of them, she was able to relax a little. She felt the worst of the ordeal was over and that they had won the Count over to their side.

She told David this, "I think he'll be very cooperative now."

The young man on the divan beside her wasn't so sure. "I hope so."

She sighed. "I've never thought him really wicked."

"You're forgetting about his weird friends and his leading them in Black Masses!"

"You don't understand how widely spread interest in the black arts is," she told him. "And most of the people who dabble in such things are quite ordinary folk. It's purely a hobby with them."

"I'll feel better after we've taken care of the vampire," David said. "If he goes through with that, I'll trust him."

"He can't back out now."

David's smile was cynical. "Never be too sure of anything. It seemed to me he gave in very suddenly at the end."

"Because he saw we were right and he doesn't want to have any scandal to hurt the family name."

The young actor nodded. "That was what was behind all this. It's strange how far these people will go for family."

Eve looked out the window. "The rain seems to be easing up," she said. "The Count spoke of a burial tonight if it did." She gave a tiny shudder. "I always wanted to delve further into witchcraft. But I didn't expect to go this far."

David took her hand in his. "By this time tomorrow we'll be on the train to Paris. This nightmare will be on its way to being forgotten."

She did not argue. But she was certain the events at the Chateau Langlais would linger much longer in her mind than the young man at her side thought. They were still sitting in the living room when the Count returned with word that Raol had already gone out in search of the hawthorn tree.

By midafternoon the rain had ended. She spent a while in her bedroom resting. As the time drew nearer for the destruction of Leonard, she became more restless. She finally decided to go downstairs, and as she walked along the landing, met Maria. The Count's wife gave no sign of seeing her but passed by staring straight ahead with a grieving expression on her strangely pale face.

Eve knew the older woman must have seen her and deliberately avoided speaking to her. She must have heard what was going on from her husband and was upset both for his sake and for the tragedy that had overtaken them all. Her attitude made Eve feel uneasy. She hoped that the Count would keep his word.

She walked through the garden to the rear of the chateau. And there in the entrance to the stables, she found David sharpening a hawthorn about an inch and a half thick. He was putting the finishing touches to the sharp point of the stake as she came up to him.

"You've found it," she said.

He glanced up at her. "Yes. Raol brought it in."

"It should do."

"I think so," David agreed. "Raol is out digging the grave now."

She grimaced. "I don't like to think about it."

"The village will be a better place to live after tonight," was David's grim comment as he put the axe aside and stood up to let her see the smooth white point of the hawthorn.

"At least a safer place," she said.

She went inside. The Count had invited David to remain at the chateau for dinner and the night, and he'd accepted. But dinner turned out to be a grim affair. Little was said and not much was eaten. They were all glad to leave the table as soon as they could. The time for the execution was drawing very close. Eve spoke with the actor briefly and then went back up to her bedroom to wait until the vampire was destroyed.

As it came nearer the fateful moment of dusk, she began to pace. She moved restlessly up and down before her window. And then, from a distance she heard a strange wailing cry that seemed to last for an unendurable time. Horror crossed her pretty face, and she pressed her hands to her ears. She stood that way for quite a little, and when she dropped her hands, silence had settled on the chateau like a heavy cloak.

She knew that it was rapidly getting dark. She wanted to go down and find out what had happened, and yet she didn't seem to be able to find the courage to leave her room. She stood there indecisively, and then an easy knock came on her door.

She opened it to see the Count standing there. His face was a mask of grief. "It's done," he said.

"It was for the good of all," she reminded him.

"We'll be burying him in the chest," the Count informed her. "David is with him now. He looks very peaceful in death. Perhaps you would care to take a last look at him before we close the top of the chest permanently."

Eve was caught in a strange predicament. She had a curiosity to see the dead vampire and yet a part of her rebelled against the idea. She had the impression the old aristocrat would like her to pay Leonard's body this last respect. Reluctantly she said she would go down.

"I'll take you there," the Count said quietly.

When they entered the stark chamber in which the chest lay, a single candle burned in a holder on the chair. Standing by the open chest was David Mazin with a grim expression on his handsome face. The young man in the rumpled gray suit showed signs of the strain he'd gone through. He turned to her, and she was shocked by his haggard appearance.

"It was over with very quickly," he told her.

"I'm glad," she said.

"You wouldn't guess he died violently," David said as she edged closer to the coffin.

She peered in briefly and was ready to agree. Leonard looked much more peaceful in death than he ever had in life. The stake still protruded from his chest. He would have to be buried that way to insure he didn't rise from the grave again.

She turned away and asked the Count, "When is the burial?"

"At once," he said. "As soon as the coffin is sealed. Will you come to the graveside?"

"Yes," she said.

It was an eerie procession. Servants of the household, including Raol, carried the coffin. Others came along with torches held high. And the Count had summoned a few of his close friends from the Satanist group to be there. They made their way through the damp grass to a tiny cemetery a short distance from the chateau.

Maria walked with the Count, David and Eve followed them, and then came Dr. Jardin and his attractive wife, Father Boulanger and some others Eve did not remember by name. At the graveside the torches were held aloft as Father Boulanger said a few words beside the coffin. The red flare of the torches brightened the dark figures around the graveside and cast a glow on the cluster of tombstones in the background. It made a weird spectacle.

Eve stood there, silently thinking of all that had taken place since the night she'd first met the Count. She fervently prayed that Leonard's soul would be at rest finally. The coffin was lowered into the ground, and then they all filed back through the foggy darkness to the chateau.

The Count shook hands with his friends at the entrance to the chateau, and then they left. When David and Eve went inside, the old man insisted that they all have some hot brandy to forestall any bad effects of the dampness. Eve was not anxious to join in, but David quietly told her he thought it might be best.

They gathered in the living room, Maria and the Count, Eve and David. The Count poured out the hot brandy himself and passed them each a glass as it came from the stout flagon. Eve felt rather guilty since the ritual seemed to suggest a toast. But the air of solemnity shown by them denied that.

The Count asked, "Are you both still determined to leave here in the morning?"

David paused with his drink. "My work requires I report in Paris. Eve can do as she pleases. If she decides to remain, I can return in a day or two."

She was startled by this change in his point of view. Previously he'd been eager to get her away from the old castle. She said, "I must go as well."

The Count looked sad. "Whatever you say. It is going to be a very different house here with all the changes. All the deaths! Isn't that so, Maria?"

His wife nodded. "Yes. I hardly know what we will do."

Eve felt embarrassed. She finished her drink and stood up. "I really must go to bed," she said. "I'll have to rise early to pack for the train."

David was also on his feet. "I'll see you to your room."

On the way up the circular stairway, she suddenly had a dizzy spell. She halted and leaned on David for support. "My head is reeling," she murmured. "I shouldn't have taken that brandy."

David gave her an understanding smile as he supported her. "It was strong, but it will do you no harm. You need a good night's rest, and this will give it to you."

"Yes," she murmured, trying to clear her head and still feeling much too light-headed for comfort. After a few seconds, the spell passed and she was able to continue up the stairs.

At the door to her room he touched his hand to her forehead and showed a worried look. "Your head is very hot. I hope you didn't get too cold and wet out there."

"I must have some fever," she acknowledged. "Your hand felt icy!"

"I hope the brandy takes care of whatever it is," David said with concern.

"I'll be all right. Now that it's over and we can finally be free." She gazed at him with loving eyes. "Goodnight, David."

"Goodnight, Eve," he said. And he took her in his arms for a parting kiss.

She went inside with her head beginning to reel again. She seemed to be burning up with an odd fever. Even the touch of David's lips had seemed different and cold. She leaned against the post of her bed and waited for the dizziness to end. But it didn't get much better.

In her unhappy condition she wasn't even able to think clearly. She somehow managed to perform the routine duties of preparing for bed. And when she was finally ready, she fell back against the pillow and drew the sheets haphazardly over her. She stared up into the shadows and had a frightening flash of clarity in which she knew she was ill or on her way to being ill. Then everything went blank.

But not for long. Nightmares came to torment her. Wild, chaotic dreams in which the bare room with the coffin in it played a terrifying part. She was down there watching from the doorway. The Count and David were moving up beside the coffin when from a distant dark corner Leonard appeared. He waited until the two were close to the coffin, and then he moved quietly across the bare room with his right hand held high. She saw the shadowy outline of a weapon in it and screamed out a warning to David. But the words did not leave her lips. There was no sound as the scream died, echoing only in her mind.

Now the vampire was directly behind David. She rushed forward to attempt to save the man she loved, but it was too late. Leonard plunged the weapon between David's shoulders, and the actor slumped down by the coffin. She sprang on the vampire and beat him with her fists, but he merely offered her a disdainful smile and pushed her roughly aside.

Count Henri Langlais stood by and watched it all without trying to interfere in any way. She was on the floor sobbing. David, clutching the side of the coffin, turned to her with a pleading expression and then slid down to the stone floor.

Leonard at once lifted him up and placed him in the coffin.

On her feet again, Eve came rushing forward, and this time Count Henri took her in his grasp as his nephew arranged David's body in the coffin. She struggled to free herself, screaming out her grief and frustration.

The Count laughed and kept repeating, "You will be a bride! You will be a bride!"

Now Leonard turned to regard her with a malevolent smile on his handsome face. He told his uncle, "Let her view the corpse."

The Count pushed her forward so she had to gaze down into the dark recesses of the coffinlike chest, and she saw the pale, rigid David in a corpse's pose. Her scream this time was one of sheer horror, for the body she was seeing was the same one the Count had taken her down to view earlier that evening!

It was David Mazin who lay in the coffin!

"Not David!" she sobbed. Then the Count roughly shoved her into the arms of the vampire. Leonard held her close, and smiling, said, "I will make you forget him!"

"No!" she screamed. "No! No!"

She awoke with her head still reeling and crying out against the embrace of the evil Leonard. And there standing at the foot of the canopied crimson bed with their faces showing concern were David, the Count and Maria.

David came to the side of the bed and bent over her urgently. He said, "You must try to relax. Count Langlais has sent for the doctor. He will be here soon."

She stared up at him with frightened eyes. "No, not the doctor," she said in a hoarse whisper. "The train! Get me away from here! Please!"

The young actor frowned. "I'm sorry, darling, but you're much too ill to think of leaving."

"I must!"

"I'll make the trip to Paris alone tomorrow," David said. "But I'll return as soon as I can. In the meantime the doctor will get you on your feet."

"David!" she pleaded.

"It will be all right," he promised. And he bent down and touched his lips to hers again.

They were like ice! It was her last thought before she slipped into a state of semi-consciousness. She tossed restlessly on the bed, dimly aware of the passage of time. Her mind was a turmoil of jumbled memory and frenzied sounds when she realized her plight. Pains racked her body, and her mouth was parched.

There were periods when she became fully aware of what was going on in the room around her, or thought she did. One of these times it was night again. The room was shadowed except for the glow of a black candle held in the hand of a sober Count Henri. The white-haired man was at her bedside, and standing with him was Maria and the horrible, parchment-faced old man, Father Boulanger. The priest bent close to her so she could see the folds of his wrinkled face like the skin of some repulsive bird of prey!

A vulture's face was the terrifying thought that passed through her mind. The unfrocked priest's sunken eyes glittered as he studied her, and she could smell the foul breath from his crumpled lips.

In a low voice he intoned: "Sang a dog with a pointed muzzle, Sang a golden-breasted marten, By his spells a hen created, Thereupon a hawk created!"

She offered a moan of protest and lifted her eyes to fix on the Count. His face was a study in sorrow. The black taper flickered, and the wax from it streaked down in tiny rivulets.

Then it was all dark velvet once more. In the distance there was a frantic mixture of voices, but she was too weary to try and distinguish among them. She was certain she knew some of them and could almost tell what they were saying, but not quite.

She was aboard the train from Paris again and moving along at a rapid rate. She was in an empty compartment and it was very silent. She wondered why she could not hear the clicking of the wheels, or why she wasn't jostled by the movement of the train over the tracks. Then suddenly the train came to a jerking halt. She opened her eyes.

The broad face of Dr. Jardin was studying her with concern. Behind him stood the Count. Dr. Jardin said, "Excellent! You are conscious again at last."

She was too weak to make any attempt to answer him. Instead she turned her head on the pillow to glance idly around the room. It was daylight, and sun was showing through the windows.

Dr. Jardin was smiling now. "The crisis has been passed. You will recover quickly."

She watched dully as the stout doctor and Count Henri conferred together in low tones. Then the doctor came back to her bedside table and opened his bag. He took out a bottle of colorless liquid and a hypodermic needle. She followed his movements with a weird fascination. He inserted the hypodermic needle in the bottle and carefully measured a dose of the watery solution.

Eve felt she had been through something like this before. And then she remembered! The pharmacy in Paris! The haunted pharmacy and the ghostly old man who'd treated her there! The double of Father Boulanger! It had been after the spider's bite and he had given her a hypo just as the doctor was preparing to do now.

Dr. Jardin gave her a benign smile. "This will do you good," he said as he swabbed her arm with alcohol before giving her the injection.

She stirred a little and tried to form the words, "You are Dr. Devereaux!" But the effort was too much. She merely lay there and felt the sharp puncture of the needle. Then the solution poured into her vein, and she immediately became drowsy.

When she opened her eyes again, it was still daylight and the Count was seated on a chair beside her. The old aristocrat was wearing a smart tweed suit that gave him an added air of distinction, and he was reading one of the leather-bound books from his library.

She lay there staring at him for a time before he realized she was awake and watching him. When he saw her eyes were open, he put down the book and turned to her with a smile.

"You're looking much better," he said.

"Was I ill?" her voice was thin and weak.

"Very ill, indeed," the Count said warmly. "Some kind of nasty virus, so Dr. Jardin claims. But he's an excellent medical man, and he's pulled you through."

"How long have I been in bed?"

"Rather a long while, I fear," the Count said sympathetically. "Exactly eight days."

She gave a small gasp of alarm. "David!"

"You need have no fears about David," the Count told her. "He made his trip to Paris and has been back again. He was very upset about you."

"Where is he now?"

"Off on another trip in connection with his film activities," the handsome, white-haired man said. "He'll be returning in a day or two."

"I want to talk to him," she said despairingly.

"And you shall," the Count promised.

"I meant to leave."

"I'm glad you didn't. Though I'm sorry you had to have this terrible illness. You must try to relax. Dr. Jardin feels you will need weeks of complete rest to return to full health. And what better place than here? It is surely quiet enough."

Eve was gradually remembering the events that had led up to her illness. Her pretty face was contorted with fear. She shook her head. "I can't stay here! Not after what happened! I keep thinking of him!"

A shadow crossed the old aristocrat's fine features. "Leonard?" he said. "He is at rest, poor fellow. I don't think you should concern yourself about him any more."

"It was all so horrible!"

"And it is over!"

She was reliving that night. "I looked into the coffin, and he seemed so peaceful. The stake still was in his body. And then the funeral! The glowing red torches and the black figures and tombstones against the crimson fog!" Her voice had gradually risen, and she sat up on an elbow, her eyes agonized.

The Count gently eased her back on the pillow. "We mustn't have any of that," he warned her. "It is exactly what the doctor doesn't want."

She closed her eyes. "When I was ill, I had dreadful nightmares."

"Nightmares?"

"Yes."

"What sort of nightmares?" His tone was soft but questioning.

"You were at my bedside holding a black candle, and that weird Father Boulanger was bent over me muttering an incantation."

The Count smiled sadly. "That was surely a bad dream. I have never brought a black candle into the room. And while poor Father Boulanger has been very concerned about you and inquired many times about your health, I have never brought him in here either."

"His horrible eyes," she said, giving the Count a frightened glance.

"He is old. But you mustn't hold that against him. He is really a very kind old man. Misunderstood by everyone from his bishop on down."

Eve frowned as other memory fragments returned. "That was not the worst of my dreams," she said.

The Count sighed. "With your high fever you were bound to have many unpleasant nightmares."

"Some of them seem so vivid."

"Indeed?"

Her eyes met his solemn gray ones. "I thought I was downstairs. At the time you and David destroyed the vampire."

"It was in your mind, of course," he said tolerantly.

"But Leonard had wakened and was out of his coffin. He was in a dark corner waiting to spring on David with a knife."

"Go on?" the old man's tone had a tenseness in it.

"I tried to cry out a warning. But the words didn't come."

"Typical of the nightmare state."

The horror of recalling it was mirrored on her pretty face. "Then Leonard killed David and placed him in the coffin. You helped him. There was nothing I could do!"

The Count smiled. "I'm glad you told me about it. You should cleanse your mind of such morbid fantasies. The whole business of the vampire was an unfair strain on you. I was mostly to blame for bringing you here and exposing you to it. But I intend to try and make it up to you."

She stared at him. "I expected you would hate me. David and I insisted on your allowing Leonard to be destroyed. We ruined all your plans."

"But I have other plans, my dear," the Count said suavely.

Chapter Eleven

The kindly attitude of Count Henri Langlais and the devoted attention of his wife, Maria, to Eve's needs helped her adjust to her convalescence at the chateau. She tried to block out all memory of Leonard from her mind. The Count had been right in saying this episode with all its horror was over. It was best forgotten. She knew she owed them all a tremendous debt for the care they'd taken of her.

Maria came to her room with a dinner tray that evening. The pale woman smiled as she sat it down on the bedside table. "Just a few simple things, my dear," she said. "Nothing heavy."

Eve was propped up in bed against several pillows. "I have no appetite."

"But you must at least have some broth. The doctor specified that you should try and take some nourishment."

"Maybe just the broth then."

"Fine," Maria said happily. And she removed the cover from the bowl with the hot liquid. "Our cook prepared this especially for you," she told Eve as she gave it to her.

Eve sipped the hot broth and found it had a pleasing if somewhat bitter taste. "It's very unusual," she said. "What's in it?"

Maria laughed lightly. "Now that is the cook's secret. She is very proud of it. But I can tell you in confidence it is a brew of herbs picked on our own estate."

"It is interesting," she said.

And she noticed that it had a good effect on her. She felt

much more comfortable after she'd taken it. The unpleasant memories did not haunt her and she relaxed. That night she had a deep, pleasant sleep and woke in the morning feeling greatly improved.

Dr. Jardin came to visit her shortly before noon. The stout man's broad face showed approval of her condition as he sat at her bedside. "In another day you will be able to get up for a little," he promised.

"I'd like that," she smiled. "I want to be on my feet when David returns."

Dr. Jardin smiled considerately. "We'll see if we can manage it."

"Just what has been wrong with me?" she asked the doctor earnestly. "Count Langlais has been rather vague about it. Is it anything I need fear will return in the future?"

The stout man sat back in the chair. "No. I'd say you'll be all right from now on. The virus you contacted must have been troubling you since that time you were first ill in Paris."

"I took ill in Dinard. You treated me there, remember?" Then she stopped and smiled apologetically. "The man who so resembled you, Dr. Devereaux was his name. You remember I was rather silly about that when we were introduced here."

Dr. Jardin nodded. "Well, that was all due to your illness. Your feeling that you were living in a nightmare world and that you'd seen some of us before. The fever kept recurring. But now I'm sure we've broken it, and it's only a matter of your mending."

"I feel I'm imposing on the Count and his wife."

"Not at all. They are lonely old people and glad to have your company."

"I suppose so," she agreed quietly. "With Therese dead and Leonard gone." She watched him for his reaction.

He acted as if he'd not heard her words. "You mustn't try to rush things," he warned. "Fight against impatience."

She decided it was a taboo subject. While he and the others belonging to the Satanist cult had known about the Count's nephew, they were not about to admit it. The doctor and his attractive young wife had attended the Black Mass burial of the century old vampire. But it was to be a closed book. Probably this was the best way to deal with it.

She said, "I'll try to be a good patient."

"When you've made some recovery, the Count can take you for a few motor rides," the Doctor said. "Brittany is a rugged but beautiful area. Some of the scenery along this coast is unique."

"I know," she said.

The stout man got up. "And eat as much as you can. We have to build you up."

"I'll try."

"Maria tells me you like the cook's special broth," Dr. Jardin said, as he picked up his medical bag.

"I do. It has a unique flavor."

"Full of good things for you," the stout man said with twinkling eyes. "I've ordered that you should have it with your dinner every night."

"Thank you," she said.

In the afternoon the Count came to sit with her for a little. She felt completely at ease with him now that the trouble between them had been settled. And she thought he looked much better than he had before her illness. There was no longer that air of tension about him, and many of the weary lines had vanished from his handsome face.

"David should return this evening," he said.

She smiled. "I'm so anxious to see him. He won't know that I'm better."

"He'll be delighted to find you so improved."

"Did you say he was somewhere near Dinard, the seaside resort where we first met?"

The Count nodded. "Yes. There is a film studio there devoted mostly to making pictures for television. He has gone to do some interviews there. He is driving back, so he could arrive any time."

"I hope he can spend a little while here," she said wistfully. "We have so much to catch up on."

"Young lovers," Count Henri said with a chuckle. "I'm sure he'll do his best to clear some time. But I must say he seems a very ambitious young man."

"He is," Eve said enthusiastically. "And I'm sure he's a very good actor."

"I talked to him a lot during your illness," the old aristocrat said. "And I have come to have a great deal of respect for him." He paused to sigh. "His likeness to Leonard is remarkable and touching. Not only in a physical way but his mental outlook seems much like my late nephew's."

"True," she said quietly.

"I suppose that has made me feel unusually close to him," the Count went on in a brisker tone. "At any rate we have come to be friends. I thought you would be pleased to hear that."

"I am," she said.

"I have talked to him about his future. And it seems to me his best opportunity might be in the field of producing and directing. This would make full use of his undoubted talents."

She smiled. "He would have to find financial backing for such a venture. He's young, and I don't think he has money of his own."

"Apparently not," said the Count. "But it shouldn't be too

hard for him to find the capital if he tried. I'd say it is something he should consider."

"How did he seem to feel about it?"

"He agreed with nearly all that I said," the Count told her with a smile. "But he is a very careful young man. He doesn't commit himself easily."

Eve was pleased with the elderly man's picture of David. She also felt he was an intelligent young man capable of doing important things. As the evening drew near and he still had not returned from Dinard, she began to feel uneasy.

Maria had made it a habit to bring up her dinner personally, though Eve had begged her not to go to this trouble. The gray-haired wife of the Count insisted it was a chore that gave her pleasure. And so, on this particular evening, as usual, she arrived with the tray.

Eve told her, "I'm too excited to eat much. The Count promised that David would be back tonight."

The woman showed a smile on her pale face and handed her the bowl of broth that had become a regular part of her diet. "At least take your broth," she said.

Eve did. And as on so many other occasions, she felt much more relaxed afterward. She even ate some of the more solid food on the tray. Maria sat by and chatted.

"The Count is having a meeting of his club tonight," she informed Eve.

"Does he have them often?"

"At least once a week," Maria said. "And then there is sometimes a reason for calling them together for special occasions."

"I see," she said.

"You must attend some of them when you're feeling better," the older woman went on. "All the members are our friends. I'd like you to know them better."

"I don't suppose I'll be here much longer," Eve reminded her. "I do have to return to Paris and the university. I have my room there."

"Of course. But while you're here I'm sure the meetings in the chapel will interest you. I didn't attend them at all in the beginning. Now I'm fascinated by all that goes on. This section of Brittany has always been strong in legend and witchcraft."

"I know," she said.

"Well, I must not tire you with my talk," Maria smiled as she got up and took the tray. "You will want to rest a little in preparation for your young man's return."

"I hope he won't be too late," Eve worried. "Your husband said David was driving back."

"We'll send him up as soon as he arrives," the Count's wife promised.

Eve rested against the pillows with her eyes closed for awhile. She was becoming increasingly edgy. Yet much of the tenseness she'd once known had left her. As an example, she no longer minded being in the chateau. The brooding atmosphere of mystery, which had made her nervous when she had first come there as a guest, didn't bother her anymore.

She finally opened her eyes, and seeing that the Count had left his book on her bedside table, she reached out and got it. There was a bookmark in it, and she opened it to that page.

She read: "Then he summons the spirits of the dead and thee who rulest the spirits of the dead and him who guards the barriers of the stream of Lethe: and he repeats the magic spell and wildly, with frenzied lips he chants a conjuration to appease or compel the fluttering of ghosts. He pours a libation of blood on the altars and burns the sacrifices entire, and soaks the trench in pools of blood."

She recognized the passage as one written by Seneca, a

Roman dramatist of the beginning of the Christian era. And what he was describing was a rite for the dead. Had the Count been reading it in preparation for the gathering of the Devil cult in the old chapel? Was he planning to offer some Black Mass for Leonard? Leonard, once Count of Langlais, now resting in the family cemetery with a hawthorn stake through his heart!

With a frown she closed the book and put it aside. Night had come, and the room was almost in darkness. Then a maid quietly entered and lit the candles on the dresser. The girl left without offering a word.

Eve heard the sound of motor cars drawing up in the driveway of the chateau. She hoped that each one might be David's car. But he did not show himself in the room and so she assumed the cars belonged to the Count's circle of black magic hobbyists. They would be gathering for their meeting. At last she heard a familiar footstep in the hall.

The next minute the door opened and David entered the room. He was wearing a blue suit and looking as handsome as ever. He smiled at her and came across the room to stand at her bedside and gaze down at her fondly.

"Eve! You've come back to yourself at last!"

She reached her hands up to take his. "I thought you would never get here," she said.

"Heavy traffic just outside Dinard," he told her. And he took her hands and sat on the bed beside her. "I was fuming all the way at the delay."

Eve took note of the weary lines in his face, and it seemed to her he was just a trifle thinner. She said, "You haven't kissed me yet."

He laughed. "I've been saving it." And without any more delay, he bent close to her and touched his lips briefly to hers. "I don't want to overdo it on this first visit since your illness."

"I'm improving every minute you're here," she said. "The doctor told me I might be able to get up tomorrow."

"Wonderful!"

She studied his handsome face with fond eyes. "Perhaps he'll even allow me to go out on the terrace and sit with you."

David hesitated. Then he said, "I'm sorry, darling. But I'll have to leave in the morning before you're awake."

"Oh, no!" she protested unhappily.

He held her hands in his. "It's just that I have this picture in production. I need to be on the set early in the morning. I really took a liberty leaving to come here for the evening."

"How disappointing! I hope the film will soon be finished."

The candlelight reflected on his handsome face, and she could see that he was concerned. "I hope so, too," he agreed. "You know how these things drag on. And I have a very good part."

Her eyes filled with tender admiration. "You know, I have never seen you act. Except when you played the part of Leonard."

"Did I do well?"

"Very well," she said with a sigh. "In many ways I was never able to tell you apart. You imitated his tone of voice and mannerisms so perfectly that I accepted them as your own."

"I'm glad you approved of my acting."

"Even now you and Leonard are mixed up in my mind," she admitted. She gave him a small pathetic smile. "But I don't worry about what happened anymore. Dr. Jardin has been treating me for this illness, and it's made the greatest change in me. I don't fret as I used to. I'm not as nervous or tense. I accept things."

"That sounds good," David said quietly.

"But I do miss you!"

"Soon I'll be with you all the time," he promised. And then with a faint smile, he added, "There is one thing I must talk to you about tonight."

"Yes?"

"I don't know how you'll feel about it," he said. "But I'll tell you in advance that it is agreeable to me. Do you understand?"

"Not really," she said. "I don't know what you're talking about."

"Count Langlais would like us to be married here as soon as you are well. Before you leave here. And I like the idea. I think the old chapel here would be a wonderfully romantic spot for a wedding."

She stared at him in astonishment. "Are you serious?"

"Yes. It seems to mean a great deal to the Count and Maria. They have offered us the use of the chapel, plus looking after all the details of the wedding. They'll even stand up with us."

"But I expected we'd be married in Paris. All my friends are there."

"So are mine," he smiled. "That's one reason I'd like to have the wedding here. I like the idea of a private wedding with only a few people. It's only important to us."

The idea was so new to her she couldn't quite grasp it. She'd taken it for granted she and David would be married, and soon. But pushing the date ahead to the point where the ceremony would take place in the chateau before she left was a startling idea.

"Do you think we should?" she asked.

He nodded. "Yes. It would make two lonely old people happy. The Count wants to do this for you as a gesture to make amends."

"It's not necessary."

David smiled. "The doctor told him that you would be well enough to be married in two weeks or so. He's anxious to start preparations. So he begged me to mention this to you tonight."

She still hesitated. "Could we invite people from Paris?"

"I think not," David said persuasively. "It would mean working on a list. Better to have a party there when we return. We can introduce each other to our friends that way."

Eve was amused at how keen he was about their being married at the chateau. She'd known he had a romantic streak, but had not expected him to come up with a suggestion like this. But she didn't really mind it. The main thing was that they were being married.

"All right," she said quietly. "You and the Count can make whatever plans you like."

"Darling!" he said with deep feeling and embraced her again.

This time his lips caressed hers a little longer than on his first kiss when he'd entered the room. And she was at once surprised to notice his lips seemed to be strangely cold.

"I hope I'm not having a fever again," she said, as he let her go. "Your lips seem so cold."

He smiled. "Probably your imagination." And then he reached into an inner pocket of the blue suit and produced a ring. "I want you to wear this from now on. I haven't had a chance to get to Paris to pick you out a ring but the Count gave me this. It's rather unusual, but few young women will have one more valuable." And he slipped it on her engagement finger.

She stared at it. "Why, it's a serpent ring!"

"Yes. Gold studded with diamonds. It's very old. The Count tells me it has been in the Langlais family for centuries and has a special significance."

Eve smiled wryly. "It's beautiful! And probably the only serpent engagement ring ever."

"These talismans have a meaning," David declared. "The Count assured me the ring would bring us good luck."

"I suppose he'd be disappointed if I didn't wear it."

"And so would I."

"Then it shall be my engagement ring," she said. And she looked at him with wondering eyes. "I can't believe it, David. We're to be married in just two weeks! What will I wear?"

"Leave that to the Count and Maria," David said happily. "I'm sure your gown will come from some famous Paris designer. And now I must go down and tell him the good news before it gets too late."

"Can't you stay with me a little longer?" she pleaded.

"I mustn't," he said. "I don't want you to have a relapse." And he got up from the bed.

"When will I see you again?"

"Some other evening," he said. "Just as soon as I can get the time off to drive back."

"Please make it soon," she begged him.

"I will," he promised.

"We have so many things to discuss," she went on excitedly. "Our honeymoon for instance. Where will we go?"

The handsome blond man laughed softly. "I think that's something for us to worry about later."

"But it is important!"

"Later," he said gently. And he touched his lips to her forehead. Then with a parting smile, he left the room and closed the door after him.

She sat there in a fog of happiness. Things were moving at a much faster pace than she'd expected. David seemed to have a new attitude towards things, and even a new authority. He was tender, but he still insisted on making the decisions.

Perhaps she wanted it that way.

The idea of having the wedding in the chapel was novel. A while ago she would have shrunk from the suggestion. But she was much more relaxed. Her room in Paris could wait. And so could her friends. She was suddenly quite content and happy here in this quiet country village.

That night she dreamed again. But her dreams were more filled with sadness than violence. She thought she and David were standing before the altar and about to be pronounced husband and wife when there was suddenly a commotion in the back of the chapel. They turned and were shocked to see Leonard marching slowly up the aisle to come between them. He was dressed the same as when she'd last seen him in his coffin. And there was a horrible stain of blood on his jacket.

Leonard came to a halt between them and in a low voice intoned, "You cannot marry! You murdered me!"

There was an uproar in the chapel, and she cried out in fear. She wakened to the darkness of her room with the cry still on her lips. And she at once realized it had been a nightmare. But what an ugly one! It was true they had conspired to destroy Leonard but for his good as well as their own. They had put his unhappy, wandering spirit to rest after a century.

Still the dream had upset her. She lay awake for some time. And it was during this period that she heard ribald laughter coming from outside by the entrance to the chapel. Then there was the sound of cars being started and driven away. After that there was a period of silence while she remained sleepless. The mournful cries of nightbirds came to haunt her.

She suddenly had an irresistable urge to get out of bed. Slowly she raised herself and slipped her legs around so her feet touched the softness of the heavy crimson rug. She did not bother to put on a robe or slippers but stood weakly. It was an experience after her long stay in bed.

Very slowly she made her way across to the nearest window and opened it. There was a large moon and the night was clear. She took a deep breath and studied the moon and the silvery reflection of it on the ocean. Then, as she continued watching, a cloud moved across the face of the moon. And there outlined was the perfect shape of a bat!

It gave her a start. And it only lasted for a moment until the cloud moved a little and the outline of it became vague. She wondered if it had been her imagination. With a tiny frown she closed the window and went back to her bed again.

She tried to go to sleep but everything seemed to bother her. The feel of the unaccustomed engagement ring on her finger was an annoyance. She pictured the sparkling diamonds of the weird serpent ring. And she had the sensation that the tiny serpent had come to life and was writhing around her finger. Alarmed she held up her hand and tried to see the ring in the darkness. Then she realized how silly this was and let her hand drop on the coverlet. At last sleep came to her again.

The second day after the evening of David's visit, Dr. Jardin allowed her to go downstairs and sit outside on the verandah. She had already been up and walking about her room the previous day and her strength had come back with remarkable swiftness. The Count now insisted on accompanying her downstairs.

"You must keep a firm hold on my arm," he advised.

"I'm really able to walk alone," she told the old aristocrat.

"I'll take no chances on the stairs," he said. "We don't want any accidents or more illness now that your wedding date has been set."

Eve was secretly amused at the excitement the Count was showing about her wedding to David. The old man had come to her the morning after David had given him the news that they would have their wedding at the chateau and told her how pleased he was. He'd promised to make the wedding a memorable event for them. Nothing in effort or money would be spared was his vow.

It was a bright, sunny morning, and she was delighted to take a seat in one of the wicker chairs on the terrace. The Count sat with her and discussed the gardens and promised the chapel would be decorated with flowers of his own growing for the wedding.

While they were talking, a bent figure in black came slowly up the driveway. It was a few minutes before Eve recognized the newcomer as the ancient Father Boulanger. She glanced at the Count.

"I had no idea he was able to get around so well," she said.

Count Henri smiled. "He's rather remarkable for his age. He often walks here from the village."

The elderly unfrocked priest made his way laboriously up the steps to the terrace. He presented a bizarre appearance in his long cassock, which was literally turning from black to green with age, his soiled clerical collar and his wide-brimmed, shabby hat. His wrinkled, yellowed face showed a smile.

"What a beautiful morning, Count," was his greeting. And to her he gave a shaky bow, saying, "Good to see you up again, Mademoiselle."

"Thank you," she said. She felt she had to tolerate the weird old man, however much he revolted her, since he was a friend of the Count.

The Count was on his feet and over by the bent priest. "What brings you this far so early in the day, Father?"

The priest gave a cackle of laughter. "I believe I left my copy of the Kalevala in the chapel last night. I am lost without it."

"We can look for it," the Count said.

The bent one gave her a cautious glance, and then leaning close to the Count, told him in his cracked voice, "Another village maiden struck down under the full moon last night! And the mark was on her throat!"

Count Henri Langlais straightened and suddenly very formal said, "I'll take you to the chapel at once." And he lost no time in leading the old man away.

It took a full moment for the import of the unfrocked priest's words to sink through to Eve. And the sudden upset registered by the Count at the news was not lost to her. Father Boulanger had surely been referring to another of the vampire attacks! This could only mean that one of the living dead was still at large in the area. But Leonard had been destroyed! She had seen thc stake lodged in his heart. Or had she been deceived? Had it been some kind of illusion? Did the evil still linger at the Chateau Langlais without her being aware of it?

For some reason she could not explain, she had an impulse to leave the terrace and go to the small cemetery just behind the chateau. There was some strong force impelling her to do this. She rose like a sleepwalker with her eyes straight ahead and went down from the terrace, through the gardens and out across a broad lawn. It was only a matter of minutes before she was within sight of the cluster of tombstones marking the cemetery.

She did not halt until she stood before the grave in which she'd seen Leonard buried. And her eyes fastened on a wide crack in the earth which covered the vampire's coffin!

Chapter Twelve

Eve continued standing there, staring at the freshly mounded grave with the wide crevice running almost the length of it. The first terrifying thought that came to her mind was: Had the vampire, Count Leonard Langlais, escaped from his grave? A grim silence hung over the bleak little cemetery as she considered this dire question.

She recalled the book the Count had been reading at her bedside the other day. It had dealt with incantations for raising the dead from their graves. And that very night there had been a meeting of the Satanists in the chapel. Had they conducted a Black Mass and invoked the vampire from the buried coffin?

In the joy she'd known at her coming marriage to David, she'd allowed all thought of the vampire to vanish from her mind. But she saw that this would never truly be possible. Always there would be the gray threat of a returning Leonard. If a girl had been attacked in the village last night and the vampire marks had been discovered on her throat, then in all likelihood her worst fears had come true. Leonard was free to threaten them again!

She had fallen into a kind of coma and stood there transfixed. All at once a hand touched her arm. She turned with a start to find herself looking into the grave face of Count Henri Langlais.

"Why have you come here?" he asked in a low voice.

Fear distorted her pretty face. "Because of him."

"Leonard?"

"Yes."

"He's in his grave covered by a good six feet of earth. You saw his corpse. Why should you come here?"

She turned to stare at the grave again. "Look at the earth. How it has fallen back. As if someone had forced his way up to the surface."

The Count's voice was cold. "Merely the action of the earth settling. It usually happens with new graves. I'll have Raol fill it in."

She gave him a questioning look. "I think he has escaped."

The Count's handsome face took on an angry look. "What has given you such morbid thoughts?"

"Father Boulanger. What he said."

"Boulanger is a silly old man," the Count said disgustedly. "I have no idea what you thought you heard. But I can promise you he said nothing about Leonard being at large."

"He said a girl was attacked. The vampire's mark was on her throat."

"I was standing with him, and I heard nothing like that," Count Henri assured her. "You must have imagined it."

Eve touched a hand to the side of her face. "I couldn't have!" But there was some uncertainty in her voice.

"You mustn't upset yourself or you'll be ill again," the old aristocrat told her. "Whatever you thought he said, you heard it wrong. Don't worry any more about it. And let us leave this sorry place."

She gave him an appealing look. "You wouldn't lie to me about this? I should know the truth."

He gave her a sad smile. "You must learn to believe I am your friend. I'll do nothing to hurt you."

She wanted to believe it. Wanted to badly. So she allowed him to lead her back to the chateau. No more was said about the vampire. But she continued to be worried that the Count had not been completely frank with her.

Dr. Jardin came in the afternoon, and while he was with her, the Count joined them. The Count gave the stout doctor a significant look and said, "I'm afraid this young lady is on the verge of nightmares again."

The doctor raised his eyebrows. "Why do you say that?"

"She had an unhappy spell this morning," the Count said. "Imagined a monstrous thing. I think she should have some kind of tonic for her nerves."

Eve half-rose in protest, a tiny panic starting within her. "I'll be all right," she promised. "It was what Father Boulanger said that upset me. I don't need medicine!"

Count Henri came and eased her back in her chair. "You mustn't become hysterical. We are all your friends. We only want to help you." And to the doctor he said, "You see how upset she is, doctor."

The stout man was reaching for his bag to open it. "I can see that," he agreed. "And I have something here that will fix her up in no time."

She turned from one to the other in distress. "I'm sure I don't need any more medicine."

"Let the doctor be the judge of that," the Count said in his kindly way.

Dr. Jardin was smiling at her. "I will leave this box of tablets. If you will take one each morning and night I think it will make a huge difference. We must have you in proper shape for the wedding."

"I want to see David," she said in a weak voice. "I need to talk to him."

"He'll be here tonight," the Count promised.

"How do you know?" she gave him a searching look. It seemed strange to her that the Count should know more about David than she did. It wasn't right.

The elderly man said, "He called me on the phone a short

time ago. I told him you weren't feeling well, and he promised to drive here this evening."

The doctor got up to go. "So you see," he said, "you have nothing to worry about." And to the Count he added, "Be sure she takes the tablets as I have ordered."

"I will," Count Henri promised. "I'll have David talk to her about the need to take them."

Eve felt she was being swept along in her weakened state. She couldn't seem to resist the stronger wills of those around her. She doubted that she needed the tablets. But she knew that she would take them to satisfy the Count. And she was sure that David, because of his new friendship with the older man, would side with him and insist she take the medication.

It turned out she was right in this. David came back to the chateau shortly after dusk. She was in the living room sitting with Maria when the young actor arrived. The Count's wife left them almost at once, and David sat on the divan with her.

"I hear you've been feeling ill again," he said, staring at her with troubled eyes.

"It was nothing," she said with a small smile. "The doctor has given me medicine for my nerves."

"See that you take it," was David's predictable advice.

She looked at him sadly. "I have missed you so," she said. "Can't you give up your film work until after the wedding? We should have some time together. These snatched hours in the evenings aren't enough for us."

He put an arm around her. "I feel exactly as you do," he said. "But I'm working for our future. There are some things you don't understand. I'd like you to go to the study with me. Count Henri is waiting there to see us."

"Must we go? I'd rather spend the time alone with you."

"Later," he said firmly. "We have to talk with the Count first."

She was surprised at his insistence but went down the shadowed corridor to the study with him. The Count was waiting for them and seemed in an unusually good humor. After they were seated he smiled at them from across his desk.

"Have you told her anything, David?" he asked.

David looking pleased, shook his head. "No, sir."

The Count told her, "I have a surprise for you. I trust you will find it a pleasant one."

There was a meaningful moment of silence in the room. She looked at the satisfied smiles of the two men and almost felt as if they were conspiring against her. But she could not believe that of David. He was her only hope. She had given him her love and trust.

"Yes?" she inquired in a small voice.

"This thing has evolved from the great fondness Maria and I have for you and David," the Count went on expansively. "We are very grateful to you for planning to have your wedding at the chateau. You are helping to dispel the loneliness of our lives."

"It is you who have been kind to us, sir," David spoke up with respect.

"I agree," Eve said.

"You are aware that David is very busy at the studios near Dinard with an important film project," the Count told her. "What you do not know is that he is working for me."

"For you?" she gasped.

The Count nodded. "Yes. I have long felt he should have the chance to prove his talent. And I wanted to offer him financial support. The purchase of this studio solved the problem. David is making his own films now, and I'm sure he'll be a success."

She turned to David, "I don't know what to say!"

David smiled. "You haven't heard it all."

"That is true," the Count agreed. "But at least you know why David is working such long hours and has to be away from you so much of the time. Now I come to perhaps the most important news of all. As you know I represent the last of the Langlais line."

"Yes," she said quietly.

"I have been greatly distressed by the thought of my estate and personal fortune passing into the hands of strangers." He paused. "So I have decided that you and David and any children you may have shall be my heirs."

Eve's eyes widened. "You are being too generous!"

The Count waved this aside with a veined hand. "I have explained my reasons. Generosity has nothing to do with it. I want to be sure the name of Langlais will live. So I have made a provision to my bequest."

"Oh?" she was puzzled by all this.

The Count got up and walked over to David and placed a hand on his shoulder. "I have asked your husband-to-be to take on my family name. I would like him to legally change his name to David Leonard Langlais."

She stared at them. "Are you serious?"

"Of course," the Count said.

David smiled at her. "You'd better not make a fuss," he warned her. "I've already agreed. It's going to be settled before the wedding. I hope you don't object to becoming Eve Langlais."

"I haven't had time to think about it," she said, her head in a whirl.

"You cannot inherit the title," the Count explained. "But it will mean that a Langlais will continue to carry on as squire in the village and live in the chateau. I am satisfied with that."

David was on his feet and facing her. "I say we should be

more than satisfied. Don't you agree, Eve? Hasn't the Count been wonderful?"

"Yes, he has," she said unsteadily. And spreading her hands, she told the two men, "I need time to realize what it all means."

The Count beamed at them. "Just don't worry about it, my dear. David and I will look after everything."

"And since this is near the studios at Dinard, I can commute morning and night and we'll be able to start our married life here," David said.

She saw the Count give her husband-to-be a warning glance, almost as if the older man were signaling him that he had said too much. The Count said, "We won't fuss over details at this time. And now that you've heard my news, I'm sure you two want to discuss it by yourselves. Don't think I'm too old to understand. So on your way, both of you!"

David took her out to the gardens where they strolled under the full moon. The night was cool, but her reasons for trembling had nothing to do with the temperature. The Count's announcement had come as a complete shock to her.

She gazed up at David's handsome profile. "You knew about this all along."

"Only for a few days."

"I wish you'd discussed it with me first," she worried.

He smiled down at her. "But what was there to discuss?"

"I don't like it," she said. "I mean you changing your name. And you're almost taking *his* name."

The blond young man halted and looked at her solemnly. "Does that seem so important to you?"

"I wanted to forget about him. We can't if you take his name."

"Forget that it was his. Think of it as mine. In time it will seem I always was David Leonard Langlais."

She found it hard to feel the way he did about it. And there were other things that bothered her. She said, "I don't know that I want to live here."

"Surely we should do this to please the Count," David said.

Eve studied him with bewildered eyes. "I don't understand you these days. You used to be so independent. Now you agree to anything the Count suggests."

"I was never before treated so generously by anyone."

"Could you be putting a price on our happiness?" she asked him solemnly.

The young actor took her by the arms. "Eve! I'm doing all this for you!"

"I hope so," she said. "I see so little of you it's like being with a stranger."

"I owe it to the Count to make a success of the film studio," David said. "I have to give it everything for the next year or two."

"The next year or two?" she demanded in despair. "What about our lives together? What about our honeymoon? We haven't made any plans."

He looked guilty. "The way it is at the studio, darling, I daren't leave now. We'll have to spend our wedding night here at the chateau and postpone our honeymoon until later."

So there it was out in the open at last. David had gained financial independence, security beyond a kind she'd ever dreamed of, but in payment for it he was being forced to surrender his personal freedom. She was to be cheated of much of his company. At the best she felt it was a dubious bargain. But knowing the change that had come over the young actor and how completely under the domination of the Count he was, she knew she would either have to agree or call off her marriage. And she loved David too much to leave him now.

The days passed quickly. She took the tablets Dr. Jardin had left, and the medication did quiet her nerves. Only now and again did she have any qualms about the fact she and David had virtually become prisoners of the suave Count Henri Langlais.

A week before her wedding day, she spoke to the old aristocrat about her room in Paris. "I have some personal things there that I would like to bring to the chateau."

His lined, handsome face showed a mocking smile. "That is all being taken care of, my dear. One of my employees in Paris is cleaning out the apartment for you, and the things will arrive here in a few days."

She was almost in tears. "But I'd have preferred to do it myself."

"Too much of a strain on you," he said soothingly. "You must rest for the important day ahead."

The following morning she had a sudden urge to talk to David. So she went to the Count's study and asked him for the studio phone number of her husband-to-be.

The Count rose from his desk with an embarrassed look. "I'm afraid I haven't got it," he said.

She stared at him. "But you told me you frequently phoned him during the day."

"By arrangement," the Count said. "He gives me a number of some cafe or office where he is going to be at a certain time and I call him there."

"You mean I can't reach David in an emergency?"

"Not as things are. There is no phone connection at the studio. All the business is transacted at an office in Dinard. David is never there as he is in charge of the actual film production. They merely send messengers back and forth between the studio and office when contact is required."

Eve was astonished and upset. "That means I'll never be able to get in touch with David in the daytime no matter what."

"Nothing is ever permanent, my dear," the old man said in his easy way. "No doubt in time the studio will have a phone. It is necessary to wait a year, sometimes two for such service because of the sad state of the telephone industry in this country. But I'm sure David has the studio on the waiting list, and there will one day be a number at which you can call him."

This ending to the interview was completely unsatisfactory to her. But when she brought it up with David that evening he told her the same story. So it seemed there was no hope.

Her crowning surprise came three days before the wedding when Maria came to her room with the wedding gown the Count had ordered from a top Parisian fashion house. The Count's wife entered Eve's bedroom with the dress over her arm.

"It has arrived at last," she said happily. "I was afraid it wouldn't come."

But Eve had frozen where she was standing, and her eyes fixed on the dress in astonishment. "But it's black!" she protested.

Maria seemed puzzled by her reaction. "That is what the Count ordered."

"A black wedding dress!" Eve said angrily. I won't wear it! A bride always wants white!"

"But I will be wearing black," the gray-haired woman argued. "And so will the doctor's wife and all the other ladies attending. That is the way it is arranged."

"Impossible!" Eve said. "It will look ridiculous! Black under the sunlight! What a mockery!"

"The wedding is to be in the chapel at midnight," Maria said with her pale face shadowed by concern. "I thought David and the Count had made it clear."

"At midnight!" Eve said incredulously. But her heart was sinking since she realized she had discussed none of these intimate details with David. It had been those tablets! They made her so drowsy and generally disinterested. She knew she shouldn't have taken them.

"I'm sorry," Maria said, holding up the dress for her to inspect. "It's too bad you're disappointed. It's such a beautiful dress."

"I don't care!" Eve said. "I'm going to talk to the Count about this." And she left Maria standing in the bedroom while she went quickly downstairs to find the Count. But he wasn't in the study or anywhere else in the main section of the chateau. She had despaired of finding him when a chance encounter with one of the maids in a side corridor gave her a clue as to his whereabouts.

"I saw him going to the west wing," the girl told her.

Eve hesitated. The west wing! She had not been there since the dreadful night when Leonard had been destroyed. For it was in the west wing the vampire had stayed. In that bare room off the luxuriously furnished living room the century-old dead man had rested in his coffin during the daylight hours. And it was from that coffin that he had risen to court her and terrorize the countryside when darkness came.

Dare she go there again? But what possible danger could there be for her there now? Summoning all her courage, she made her way along the cold, dark corridor to the distant wing. She found the oak door ajar and went on into the apartment that had been occupied by Leonard. There was no sign of the Count in the big living room. Her eyes wandered to the door leading to the dark, unfurnished room where the vampire had slept in his coffin. Dare she venture nearer and look inside?

She hesitated a moment before moving on. She reached the door and forced herself to peer inside the shadowed room. And Count Henry Langlais was standing there with his head bowed. He did not see her as his back was to the doorway. But her eyes had wandered beyond him, and in the dark corner where the vampire's coffin had once rested, there was another smaller but more elaborate casket. The coincidence of it made her gasp aloud.

Count Henri looked up suddenly, and seeing who it was, came hurriedly towards her. "What are you doing here?" he demanded harshly.

"I was looking for you," she said. And her frightened eyes left him to fix on the casket. "What does that mean?"

"You shouldn't have followed me!" the old man said angrily. "You have no right to be here!"

"The casket," she repeated dully, "what does it mean?"

He stared at her for an angry moment. Then he shrugged. "If you must know, it is mine."

"Yours?"

"Yes. Does it surprise you so that a man should want to choose his own casket? They are not available in this isolated place. Not such fine ones as this. I ordered it from Paris, and I have stored it here."

"It's where he used to be."

The Count shrugged. "That has nothing to do with it. I wanted it kept out of the way where my wife wouldn't see it. And yet I hesitated to keep it in the cellar where it would be covered by filth and cobwebs in no time. So I have installed it here."

"I'm sorry," she said. "I didn't mean to intrude."

He eyed her sternly. "This is not a healthy place for you. I want your solemn word that you will not come here again."

"I'm not likely to," she said.

"Let us leave at once," the Count said, taking her arm.

When they reached the main house, she told him her feelings about the black gown and her wedding at midnight. He seemed as astonished as his wife had been.

"But I did it for you!" he exclaimed.

"For me?"

"My group members and myself have gone to a great deal of expense and trouble to make this a truly memorable occasion for you," he said. "We plan to begin the ceremony with a ritual used in weddings in Satanic circles in this area years ago. We will reproduce the ceremony in every detail. It is a tribute to you as a student of the black arts."

"I would have preferred an ordinary wedding," she demurred.

"I fear it is too late to change things now," he said in his suave way.

So on the appointed midnight the ceremony was held in the dimly lighted chapel. Black candles flickered at the altar and in the wall brackets of the vaulted gothic hall. The Count's friends were all there dressed in the deepest of black. And it was the stooped Father Boulanger who intoned the wedding ceremony in his cracked voice. The Count explained to Eve that the old man had been given special permission to perform the service.

She had been put on a heavier dose of those helpful tablets by Dr. Jardin, and so she had quietly gone along with all the arrangements. In her lovely dark gown she looked very young and pale, and perhaps a trifle frightened. At her side David stood proud and happy. He gave her a reassuring smile as he placed the wedding ring on her finger.

The organ began to play softly in the background. And

Father Boulanger raised a claw-like hand and began to murmur an incantation in words she did not understand. The words were taken up in a chant by the others of the Satanic circle in the body of the chapel. They became a sort of wailing. She glanced at her new husband, and in the shadows he seemed to have suddenly taken on an old, haggard appearance.

It was frightening. Then he turned to her and smiled, and the illusion was broken. He looked his handsome self again. They turned and walked down through the chapel with the members of the Devil's Circle smiling at them approvingly.

All in all her wedding night was a happy one. Eve was satisfied that David loved her. And because of this she was content that he should leave her during the daylight hours for his pressure of work at the film studios and never return before dusk. She adjusted herself to this routine, and life at the chateau became a pleasant and uneventful experience.

The months went by swiftly and soon it was spring again. The chateau had become Eve's home, and she thought little of Paris and rarely wrote her family in America. When David was with her in the evenings and nights, she was never lonely, though once or twice during a month he would often have to be away for several nights at a time. She dreaded these occasions and always took strong doses of a sleeping potion Dr. Jardin had given her when she had to face the darkness by herself.

The fact that she had become isolated from the village and the outside world in general did not disturb her. The castle grounds were lovely in all seasons and the chateau itself an enchanted place. And both the Count and Maria had been extremely kind to her. She had become a member of the Satanist group and attended their meetings regularly. And she was continuing her studies in the black arts independently.

The Count had made her a present of a large black cat who became her almost constant companion. She called him Satan. On a pleasant night in May when her husband had joined her shortly after dusk, she broke the good news to them all.

"The name of Langlais is not to die out after all," she told the Count with a smile. "I'm going to have a baby."

"Bless you, my dear," the Count said and kissed her.

Maria also kissed her and said, "How wonderful!"

David merely smiled at her in his proud way and said, "I think we should enjoy this alone. Let's take a walk along the cliffs."

And they did. Hand in hand. He told her of his deep love for her and of this being the happiest moment of his life. It was nearly dark, and as they reached a high point he stopped and turned from her to stare out across the water.

She was startled. "Can you see anything?" she asked.

"Yes," he said, still studying the shadowed horizon. "I have unusual eyesight. I do very well in the darkness."

Her eyes fixed on him in bewilderment. "You sound just like him!"

David turned to her with a smile. "Just like whom?"

"You know. Leonard."

He shook his head. "You're imagining things again."

"No," she insisted. "Several times when I walked here with him he stopped and stared out at the ocean just as you were doing now. And he said he could see after dark. Sometimes I think since you took his name you've grown to be like him."

He came close to her. Taking her by the arms he smiled, "It really doesn't matter. You always were getting us mixed up."

"Yes, I did have trouble."

"Things will be better when we have our son," he told her.

She smiled. "How can you be sure it will be a son?"

"I'm sure," he said confidently. "And I've already decided on his name."

"Tell me?"

"David Leonard Langlais," he said. And he kissed her. It was strange. She no longer thought about his lips being so icy cold.